THE QUARRY

Books

THE JUDGE AND HIS HANGMAN
THE PLEDGE
TRAPS

Play

THE VISIT

Translated from the German by
EVA H. MORREALE

THE QUARRY

FRIEDRICH DUERRENMATT

NEW YORK GRAPHIC SOCIETY

GREENWICH, CONNECTICUT

1962

LIBRARY OF CONGRESS CATALOG CARD NO. 62–7252

© NEW YORK GRAPHIC SOCIETY 1961

FIRST PUBLISHED IN "ESQUIRE," MAY, 1961

FIRST PUBLISHED IN BOOK FORM 1962

PRINTED IN THE UNITED STATES OF AMERICA

PUBLISHED SIMULTANEOUSLY IN CANADA BY
LONGMANS CANADA, LIMITED, TORONTO

THE QUARRY

FIRST PART

In the beginning of November, 1948, Commissioner Barlach had been committed to the Salem—the hospital from which one looks down on the old city of Bern and its town hall. A heart attack had delayed the urgent operation for two weeks. When the difficult task was finally undertaken, it was performed successfully, but the pathological report showed the hopeless disease the doctors had suspected. Things looked grim for the Commissioner. His boss, Dr. Lutz, had twice now expected his death, and had twice been given new hope, when, finally, shortly before Christmas, improvement set in. The old man slept through the holidays, but on the twenty-seventh, a Monday, he was awake and looking at old issues of *Life* magazine from the year 1945.

"They were beasts, Samuel," he said that evening, when Dr. Hungertobel entered the room to make his visit. "They were beasts," and he handed him the magazine. "You as a doctor can fully comprehend it. Look at this picture from the Stutthof concentration camp! The camp doctor Nehle is performing a stomach opera-

3

tion on an inmate without anesthesia, and somebody photographed him."

"The Nazis did that sometimes," said the doctor, and looked at the picture. He turned pale just as he was about to throw it aside.

"What's the matter?" the sick man asked, surprised.

Hungertobel did not reply immediately. He dropped the open magazine on Barlach's bed, reached in the right upper pocket of his white coat, and pulled out a pair of horn-rimmed glasses. The Commissioner noticed that his hands shook when he put them on. Then he looked at the picture a second time.

Why is he so nervous? thought Barlach.

"Nonsense!" Hungertobel finally said angrily, and put the magazine on the table with the others. "Come, let me have your hand. We want to check your pulse."

There was silence for a minute. Then the doctor let go of his friend's arm and looked at the chart over the bed.

"You're doing fine, Hans."

"One more year?" Barlach asked.

Hungertobel was embarrassed. "We won't talk about that now," he said. "You'll have to be careful and come in for checkups."

"I'm always careful," scoffed the old man.

"That's fine," said Hungertobel, and bade him good-by.

"Give me that *Life*," the sick man said, in a seem-

4

ingly bored tone. Hungertobel gave him a magazine from the pile on the night table.

"Not that one," said the Commissioner, and looked scornfully at the doctor. "I want the one you took away from me. I'm not that easily diverted from a concentration camp."

Hungertobel hesitated for a moment, blushed when he saw Barlach's inquisitive glance, and handed him the magazine. Then he left quickly, as if there was something that distressed him. A nurse entered. The Commissioner had the other magazines removed.

"How about this one?" asked the nurse, and pointed to the magazine lying on Barlach's blanket.

"No, not this one," said the old man. After the nurse had left, he scrutinized the picture again. The doctor who was conducting the ghastly experiment appeared in his calm like a terrible god. Most of his face was hidden under the surgical mask.

The Commissioner carefully put the magazine into the drawer of the table and folded his arms behind his head. His eyes were wide open, and he watched the night which more and more filled the room. He did not turn on the light.

Later the nurse came with food. It was still not much and still part of a diet—oatmeal soup. He did not touch the lime-blossom tea, which he loathed. After he had finished the soup, he turned out the lights and looked again into the darkness, into the impenetrable shadows.

He loved to watch the lights of the city fall through the window.

When the nurse came to prepare the Commissioner for the night, he was already asleep.

Around ten o'clock in the morning, Hungertobel came.

Barlach was lying in bed, hands behind his head, and on the blanket was the magazine—opened. His eyes searched the doctor. Hungertobel saw that it was the picture from the concentration camp the old man had in front of him.

"Won't you tell me why you turned pale as death when I showed you this picture in *Life?*" the sick man asked.

Hungertobel stepped to the bed, took down the chart, studied it more carefully than usual, and hung it back in its place. "It was a ridiculous error, Hans," he said, "not worth mentioning."

"Do you know this Doctor Nehle?" Barlach's voice sounded strangely aroused.

"No," answered Hungertobel. "I don't know him. He just reminded me of somebody."

"The resemblance must be great," said the Commissioner.

The doctor admitted that the resemblance was great, and again looked at the picture. And again he was upset, as Barlach could clearly observe. But the photograph only showed half the face. "All doctors look alike when they operate," Hungertobel said.

6

"Whom does that beast remind you of?" the old man insisted without pity.

"But it doesn't make sense," answered Hungertobel. "I've already told you it must be a mistake."

"Nevertheless—you'd swear it was he, wouldn't you, Samuel?"

"Well, yes," replied the doctor. He would swear to it were it not for the fact that it could not be the man he suspected. They were better off leaving well enough alone. It was not a particularly good idea to thumb through old *Lifes* right after an operation which had been a matter of life and death.

"That doctor there," he continued after a pause, looking at the picture again as if hypnotized, "could not be the one I knew, because the doctor I knew was in Chile during the war. So the whole thing is nonsense, anybody can see that."

"In Chile, in Chile," said Barlach. "When did he return, this doctor of yours who could not possibly be Nehle?"

"In forty-five."

"In Chile, in Chile," Barlach repeated. "And you don't want to tell me who this picture reminds you of?"

Hungertobel hesitated. The whole affair was very painful to the old doctor.

"If I tell you the name, Hans," he finally volunteered, "you'll become suspicious of the man."

"I *am* suspicious of him," answered the Commissioner.

7

Hungertobel sighed. "You see, Hans," he said, "that's what I was afraid of. I don't want it, do you understand? I'm an old doctor and I don't wish to harm anybody. Your suspicion is sheer insanity. You can't just suspect somebody on account of a mere photograph, especially if it shows so little of his face. And besides, he was in Chile. That's a fact."

"What was he doing there?" the Commissioner interrupted.

"He directed a clinic in Santiago," said Hungertobel.

"In Chile, in Chile," Barlach repeated again. "That's a fascinating refrain and a difficult fact to check. You're right, Samuel, suspicion is something terrible and comes from the devil. Nothing makes man as evil as suspicion," he continued. "I know it, and I've often cursed my profession for it. A man shouldn't ever have to think like that. But now I do have a suspicion, and you gave it to me. I'd like to give it back to you, old friend, if you were able to forget it yourself. But you're the one who can't shake it off."

Hungertobel sat down on the bed. Helplessly he looked at the Commissioner. The sun fell through the window. It was a beautiful day outside, as so often in this mild winter.

"I cannot," the doctor finally said into the silence of the sickroom. "I cannot. God help me, I cannot get rid of the suspicion. I know him too well. I studied with

8

him, and twice he took over my practice for me. It's him in the picture—even the scar above the temple from the operation is there. I know it, I operated on Emmenberger myself."

Hungertobel took off his glasses and put them in his right upper pocket. Then he wiped the perspiration off his forehead.

"Emmenberger?" the Commissioner asked calmly after a while. "Is that his name?"

"Now I've said it," Hungertobel answered distressed. "Fritz Emmenberger."

"A medical doctor?"

"A medical doctor."

"And he lives in Switzerland?"

"He owns the clinic Sonnenstein on the Zurich mountain," answered the doctor. "In thirty-two he emigrated to Germany and then to Chile. In forty-five he returned and took over the clinic. One of the most expensive clinics in Switzerland," he added in a low voice.

"Only for the rich?"

"Only for the very rich."

"Is he a good scientist, Samuel?" asked the Commissioner.

Hungertobel hesitated. Finally he said that it was difficult to answer that question. "At one time he was a good scientist, only we don't really know whether he remained one. His methods appear questionable to us. As yet, we still know dishearteningly little about the hormones in which he specializes. All kinds of people are invading his field, as in any about to be conquered by science. Scientists and quacks—often combine in one person. But then, what do you want, Hans? Emmenberger is liked by his patients, and they believe in him as they do in God. To me, that seems the most important point for such wealthy clients who want even their illnesses to be a luxury. Nothing can be accomplished without faith—least of all when it involves hormones. So he has success, is loved, and makes money. After all, why else would we call him the 'heir apparent'?"

Hungertobel suddenly stopped talking, as if he regretted having uttered Emmenberger's nickname.

"The heir apparent. Why that nickname?" asked Barlach.

"The clinic has inherited the fortunes of many patients," answered Hungertobel, obviously plagued by a bad conscience. "Willing one's estate to it seems to be the fashionable thing to do there."

"So you doctors noticed this?" said the Commissioner.

The two did not speak. The silence bore something unspoken, of which Hungertobel was afraid.

"You mustn't think what you're thinking," he suddenly exclaimed, horrified.

"I'm only thinking your thoughts," answered the Commissioner calmly. "We want to be precise. What we're thinking may be criminal—yet, we ought not to be afraid of our thoughts. Only if we admit them to our consciousness can we test them and—if we're wrong— overcome them. What *are* we thinking now, Samuel? We're thinking that Emmenberger forces his patients to leave him their fortunes. He forces them by methods he learned in the Stutthof concentration camp. And later he kills them."

"No!" Hungertobel cried with feverish eyes. "No!" Helplessly he stared at Barlach. "We mustn't think that! We're not beasts!" he called again, and jumped up to pace around the room, from the wall to the window, from the window to the bed.

"My God," groaned the doctor. "This is one of the most terrible hours of my life."

"Suspicion," said the old man in the bed, and then once more, mercilessly, "suspicion."

Hungertobel stopped at Barlach's bed. "Let's forget this talk, Hans," he pleaded. "We went too far. Naturally, we all like to play around with possibilities at times. But it's bad. Let's drop Emmenberger. The more I see the photograph, the less it looks like him—honestly, I'm not making up an excuse. He was in Chile and not in Stutthof, and so our suspicion is senseless."

"In Chile, in Chile," said Barlach, and his eyes sparkled greedily for a new adventure. He stretched his body, then he lay motionless and relaxed, hands behind his head.

"You must go to your patients now, Samuel," he said

after a while. "They're waiting for you. I don't wish to detain you any longer. Let's forget our talk. You're right, it's best this way."

When Hungertobel, on his way out, suspiciously turned toward the sick man, the Commissioner was already asleep.

THE ALIBI

THE next morning at seven-thirty Hungertobel found the old man studying the *City Gazette*. He was surprised, for the doctor had come earlier than usual and Barlach was usually asleep again at this hour or at least dozing, his hands behind his head. Also, it seemed to the doctor that the Commissioner was friskier, and the old vitality seemed to gleam in his eyes.

"How're you doing?" Hungertobel greeted the sick man.

He was sniffing the morning air, was the evasive answer.

"I came earlier than usual, and I'm not really here officially," said Hungertobel and stepped to the bed. "I'm just bringing a heap of medical journals. The *Swiss Medical Weekly*, a French one and, since you understand English, too, a number of issues of *Lancet*, the famous British medical journal."

13

"It's ever so nice of you to assume I'm interested in this stuff," answered Barlach, without looking up from the *Gazette*, "but I don't know that it's quite the proper literature for me. You know perfectly well I'm no friend of medicine."

Hungertobel laughed. "And that from somebody we've helped."

"Well," said Barlach, "that doesn't make it any less of a nuisance."

Hungertobel asked him what he was reading in the *Gazette*.

"Advertisements for stamps," answered the old man.

The doctor shook his head. "Nevertheless, you'll look at these journals, even though you generally won't have anything to do with us doctors. I'm determined to prove that our talk yesterday was folly, Hans. You're a criminologist and I feel you're capable of having our fashionable doctor and all his hormones arrested out of a clear blue sky. I can't understand how I could have forgotten it. It's easy enough to prove that Emmenberger was in Santiago. He published articles from there in various medical journals, including British and American ones, mostly concerning questions of internal secretion, and made a name for himself. Even as a student he had distinguished himself as a writer with a witty and brilliant style. As you can see, he was a competent and conscientious scientist. His present leaning toward the fashionable, if I may call it that, is all the more regrettable; for what he's doing now is distinctly questionable, any way you look at it. The last article appeared in *Lancet* in January of forty-five, a few months before his return to Switzerland. That's certainly evidence that our suspicion was regular idiocy. I promise you solemnly never again to play criminologist. The man in the picture cannot be Emmenberger, or the photograph is forged."

"That would be an alibi," said Barlach, and folded the newspaper. "You may leave those journals."

When Hungertobel returned around ten for his regular visit, the old man was lying in bed, diligently reading the journals.

"Medicine does seem to interest you all of a sudden," the doctor said, surprised, and checked Barlach's pulse.

The Commissioner said that Hungertobel was right. The articles did come from Chile.

Hungertobel was happy and relieved.

"You see! And we already had Emmenberger a mass murderer!"

"Mankind has made the most astonishing advances in that art today," Barlach answered dryly. "Progress, my friend, progress. I don't need the English journals, but leave the Swiss ones here."

"But Emmenberger's articles in *Lancet* are much more important," contradicted Hungertobel, convinced that his friend really was interested in medicine. "They're the ones you must read."

"But in the *Swiss Medical Weekly* Emmenberger writes in German," Barlach retorted rather ironically.

"And?" asked the doctor, who understood nothing.

"I mean that I'm occupied with his style, Samuel, the style of a doctor who once wrote with elegance and now writes in a most awkward manner," said the old man cautiously.

And what did that indicate, asked Hungertobel, still unsuspecting, busy with the chart above the bed.

"It's not that easy to furnish an alibi," said the Commissioner.

"What are you driving at?" the doctor explained, thunderstruck. "You mean you still haven't gotten over your suspicion?"

Thoughtfully Barlach looked into the face of his dismayed friend—into this old, noble, wrinkled doctor's face. He was a doctor who had never in his life taken his patients lightly, yet knew nothing about human beings. And then he said: "You're still smoking your 'Little Rose of Sumatra,' Samuel, aren't you? It would be nice if you offered me one. I imagine it would be very pleasant to light one after my boring oatmeal soup."

THE DISCHARGE

But before lunch was served, the sick man, who had been reading Emmenberger's article about the pancreas over and over, received his first visitor since the operation. It was the "boss," who came in around eleven o'clock and nervously sat down by the bed, without taking off his overcoat, holding his hat in his hand. Barlach knew exactly the meaning of this visit, and the boss knew exactly how things were going for the Commissioner.

"Well, Commissioner," Lutz began, "how are you? For a while there we had to expect the worst."

"It's coming along slowly," answered Barlach, and clasped his hands behind his neck.

"What are you reading?" Lutz asked. He disliked coming to the point of his visit and was looking for a diversion. "Well, what do you know, medical journals."

The old man was not embarrassed. "It reads like a detective story," he said. "You try to widen your horizon when you're sick and look for new fields."

17

Lutz wanted to know how long, in the doctors' opinion, Barlach would be bedridden.

"Two months," the Commissioner answered, "I'm supposed to stay put for two months."

Whether he wanted to or not, the boss had to tackle it now. "The age limit," he stuttered. "The age limit, Commissioner. You understand. We can't get around it, you know, we have to obey the laws."

"I understand," answered the sick man. His face was expressionless.

"What has to be done, has to be done," said Lutz. "You will have to take it easy, Commissioner, and that's another reason."

"And my attitude about 'modern scientific criminology,' where one finds the criminal as if he were a jar of name-brand marmalade—that has nothing to do with it?" said Barlach, correcting Lutz. Who was to be his successor, he wanted to know.

"Rothlisberger," answered the boss. "He's substituting for you now."

Barlach nodded. "Rothlisberger. Well, with his five children, he'll be glad of the higher salary," he said. "Starting at the New Year?"

"Starting at the New Year," acknowledged Lutz.

"Till Friday then," said Barlach. "And from then on I'll be the ex-Police Commissioner." He was glad to be through with serving the state. Not because he would have more time now to read Molière and Balzac, though that would be wonderful. No, the main reason remained the fact that something was wrong with the nice, simple, homely order of the world. He knew, he had found out. People were always the same, whether they went to the Hagia Sophia in Istanbul or the Cathedral in Bern on Sundays. The big criminals were running free while the small ones were stuck in jails. And anyway, there were all kinds of crimes nobody paid any attention to, only because they were more aesthetic than some sensational murder which gets into the headlines. But actually they were both the same, provided you looked at the facts and had the imagination.

Imagination, there was the crux of the matter, imagination! Out of sheer lack of imagination a good, upstanding businessman will—between his *apéritif* and lunch—commit a crime by closing some shrewd deal. A crime of which nobody has a notion, least of all the businessman, because nobody has the imagination to see all its consequences. The world was bad out of slovenliness, and well on the way to going to the devil out of slovenliness. This was a danger bigger than Stalin and all the other Joes taken together. The civil service was no longer the place for an old hunting dog like him. Too much petty stuff, too much snooping. But the worth-while game, the game that should be hunted, the really big beasts, were under the protection of the state, like beasts in a zoological garden.

Dr. Lutz looked angry when he heard this sermon.

19

He found it most objectionable, and actually he thought it improper not to protest against such immoral attitudes. But after all, the old man was sick and would very soon retire. Thank God. Unfortunately, he had to go now, he said, swallowing his anger, he was due at a meeting of the Public Welfare Office at eleven-thirty.

The Public Welfare Office was another place that had more to do with the police than the Finance Department, commented the Commissioner. A lot was wrong there, too. Lutz prepared himself for the worst, but to his relief Barlach switched to something else. "You can do me a favor now that I'm sick and no longer useful."

"Gladly," promised Lutz.

"You see, I'd like some information. I'm curious by nature, and I'm amusing myself in my bed here with criminological combinations. An old cat just cannot give up chasing mice. In this issue of *Life* I found a picture of an SS camp doctor in Stutthof by the name of Nehle. Try to find out whether he is still in jail or what became of him. We have the international service for these cases, and it won't cost us anything since the SS has been declared a criminal organization."

Lutz wrote everything down. He would inquire, he promised, surprised at the old man's request. Then he said good-by.

"Good luck, and get well," he said, shaking the Commissioner's hand. "I'll have the information for you by tonight. Then you can speculate to your heart's delight. By the way, Blatter's here, and would like to say hello. I'll wait in the car."

So the big fat Blatter came in and Lutz disappeared.

"Greetings, Blatter," said Barlach to the policeman who had so often been his chauffeur. "I'm glad to see you."

"So am I, so am I," said Blatter. "We miss you, Commissioner. We miss you very much."

"Well, Blatter, now Rothlisberger will take my place and change the tune, I suppose," answered the old man.

"Pity," said the policeman. "Well, I don't mean him any harm, and I guess he'll do. If only you get well again."

Barlach asked whether Blatter knew the old bookstore in the Matte, the one that was owned by the Jew with the white beard, Feitelbach?

Blatter nodded. "The one with the display of stamps that never changes in the window."

"Please drop by there this afternoon and tell Feitelbach to send me *Gulliver's Travels*. It's the last service I'll ask of you."

"The book about the dwarfs and the giants?" wondered the policeman.

Barlach laughed, "Well, you see, Blatter, I adore fairy tales."

Something in this laugh struck the policeman as sinister, but he dared not ask questions.

THE HUT

By evening Lutz had already called. Hungertobel
had just sat down beside his friend's bed. He had ordered
a cup of coffee, for he had to operate later and he wanted
to take this opportunity of having his friend "for himself."
Now the phone rang and interrupted their conversation.

Barlach picked it up and listened intently. After a
while he said, "That's good enough, send me the ma-
terial," and hung up. "Nehle's dead," he explained.

"Thank God!" Hungertobel exclaimed. "Come on,
let's celebrate," and he lit a "Little Rose of Sumatra." "I
hope the nurse won't come just now."

"She certainly didn't like it at noon," Barlach said.
"I had to say you gave me permission to smoke, and she
said that sounded just like you."

"When did Nehle die?" asked the doctor.

"In forty-five, on the tenth of August. He committed suicide in a hotel in Hamburg, with poison."

23

"You see"—Hungertobel nodded—"now the rest of your suspicion has gone up in smoke."

Barlach blinked at the smoke clouds which Hungertobel delightedly puffed in rings and spirals. Nothing was as resistant to going up in smoke as suspicion, because nothing kept materializing again as quickly, he answered finally.

"You're incorrigible." Hungertobel laughed; he now looked on the whole affair as a harmless joke.

"The first virtue of a criminologist," replied the old man. And then he asked, "Samuel, were you a friend of Emmenberger's?"

"No," answered Hungertobel, "I wasn't, and as far as I remember, none of us who studied with him was. I've thought about this whole thing—the picture in *Life* and so on—again and again, Hans. I'll tell you how it happened that I thought this monster of an SS doctor might be Emmenberger—undoubtedly you've wondered. After all, one can't tell much from the picture, and my mistake must stem from something different besides a mere resemblance, even though that exists. I hadn't thought about the story for a long time, not only because it lies far back, but even more because it was horrible. And we all like to forget experiences that frightened us. I was present once, Hans, when Emmenberger performed an operation without anesthesia, and for me it was a scene from hell, if there is such a place."

"There is," Barlach answered quietly. "In other

24

words, Emmenberger did do something like this once—something like what we suspected him of?"

"You see," said the doctor, "there was no alternative at the time. The poor devil who was operated on is still alive. If you ask him about it, he'll swear by all that's holy that Emmenberger is a devil. And that's unjust, for without Emmenberger he'd be dead. But to tell you the truth, I can understand him. It was horrible."

"How did it happen?" Barlach asked.

Hungertobel drank the last drop from his cup and lit his "Little Rose" again. "Frankly, it was no magic. There's no room for magic in medicine. It didn't take more than a pocketknife and courage, and, of course, knowledge of anatomy. But who of us young students had the necessary presence of mind?

"Five of us, all medical students, had climbed from Kienvalley into the Blümlisalp region. I don't remember where we were going. I've never been a great mountain climber, and I'm an even worse geographer. I suppose it was some time in nineteen eight, probably July. And it was a hot summer, that I recall. We stayed overnight in a hut on one of the Alps. It's strange that I should recall that hut so vividly. Sometimes I dream of it, and I wake up, bathed in perspiration. Yet it was probably no different from any other such hut, and the horror attached to it for me exists only in my fantasy. That this must be so, I realize when I remember that I always visualize it covered with damp moss, and in reality you don't find moss on mountain huts. I've sometimes read of knackers' huts without really knowing what was meant. Well, when I see the words 'a knacker's hut,' I imagine something like this one. It was surrounded by fir trees and had a well not far from the door. It was of wood, not black, but white and rotten—but that, too, I may have imagined afterward. So many years lie between today and this occurrence that dream and reality are inseparably woven together.

"But I recall very clearly the nebulous fear that struck me when we approached the hut, crossing a stony meadow. I'm convinced this fear gripped all of us, except Emmenberger, perhaps. Our talk died down. The evening sun, which sank before we reached the hut, made the scene all the more frightful, since a strange deep-red light settled for an almost unbearable length of time on this empty world of ice and stone. It was a deathly illumination, tinting our faces and hands, an illumination appropriate for a planet that revolves around the sun at a far greater distance than ours.

"Like hunted animals we stormed into the hut. Its door was unlocked. The inside was poor and bare, furnished with nothing more than a few bunks. But in the faint light we saw some straw under the roof. A black crooked ladder, covered with a year's dirt, led up to it. Emmenberger fetched water from the well with a strange haste, as if he knew what was going to happen. Needless to say, that's impossible. We started a fire on the primitive stove; there was even a kettle. And then, in this weird atmosphere of fear and fatigue which had overcome us, one of us met with an accident. It was a fat boy from Lucerne, the son of an innkeeper—nobody really knew why he was studying medicine. A year later he took over his father's hotel. He was an awkward fellow. He had climbed the ladder to reach the straw under the roof. When the ladder suddenly collapsed, he fell clumsily, hitting his neck against a protruding beam, and lay moaning on the floor. It was a bad fall! At first we thought he'd broken something, but soon he started to gasp for breath. We had carried him outside to a bench, and he lay there in the strange light of the sinking sun which shone down from towering cloud banks. The sight of the hurt boy was frightening. His throat bore bloody scratches and was swollen, he held his head back, while the larynx seemed to convulse. Horrified, we noticed his face turn darker and darker, almost black in the infernal shimmer from the horizon, and his wide-open eyes gleamed like two wet white pebbles.

"We struggled desperately with cold compresses. In vain. His throat swelled more and more internally, and he threatened to choke. At first he had been filled with a feverish tension, but now he was apathetic. His breath hissed, he could no longer speak. We knew that his life was in extreme danger; we were helpless. We lacked experience and probably knowledge. We knew that there was an emergency operation which would help but nobody dared to think about it. Only Emmenberger understood and did not hesitate to act. He examined the Lucerner, disinfected his pocketknife in the boiling water on the stove, and then performed a cut we call a tracheotomy, which in emergencies sometimes has to be performed; it involves making a cut above the larynx in order to get an air passage. The operation wasn't what was so terrifying, Hans—it had to be done with a pocketknife. No, the horror was in something different—something that took place between those two, in their faces. Though the injured boy was almost unconscious from lack of air, his eyes were open, very wide open, and so he had to observe all that happened, even though maybe as if in a dream. And when Emmenberger made that cut, my God, Hans, his eyes were wide open, too, and his face distorted. All of a sudden it seemed as if something satanic broke out of those eyes, a kind of overwhelming joy of torture—or whatever you want to call it. For a second I felt a paralyzing fright, but only for a second—then it was over. But I believe I was the only one to feel it—the others did not dare to watch. I believe, too, that part of what I experienced is in my imagination only, that the sinister hut and the uncanny light contributed to the illusion.

"The strange thing about the incident is, though, that the Lucerner whose life Emmenberger had saved never spoke to him again. He hardly thanked him, which a lot of people resented. Emmenberger, on the other hand, became quite a celebrity. His career was strange. We had all thought he would make a name for himself, but fame did not attract him. He studied a lot and in a wild fashion. Physics, mathematics—nothing seemed to satisfy him. He was even seen in lectures on philosophy and theology. He passed his examinations brilliantly, but never practiced. He worked as a substitute—for me, among others—and I must admit, patients were enthusiastic about him—with the exception of a few who did not like him. He led a restless and lonely life, until he finally emigrated. He published strange articles, for instance one about the justification for astrology, one of the most sophistical things I ever read. As far as I know, he hardly ever saw anybody and became a cynical, unreliable character, all the more unpleasant because nobody felt capable of handling his sarcasm. What surprised us was the great change in Chile, that he did such sober and scientific work—it must have been the climate or the surroundings. Of course, once he returned to Switzerland, he became exactly what he had been before."

"I hope you saved the article on astrology," said Barlach when Hungertobel had finished.

The doctor answered that he could bring it to him tomorrow.

"So this is the story," the Commissioner went on thoughtfully.

"As you can see," said Hungertobel, "maybe I did spend too much of my life dreaming after all."

29

"Dreams don't lie," replied Barlach.

"Dreams lie most of all," said Hungertobel. "But you'll have to excuse me, I have to operate." And he rose from his chair.

Barlach gave him his hand. "Not a tracheotomy, I hope, or whatever you call it."

Hungertobel laughed. "A ruptured groin, Hans. I like that better even though it is more difficult. But you must rest now. What you need most is twelve hours of sleep."

GULLIVER

BUT around midnight the old man awakened when a soft noise came from the window and the cold night air rushed in.

The Commissioner did not turn on the lights at once. Instead, he pondered what was happening. He guessed that the shutters were slowly being pushed up. The darkness that surrounded him lifted; phantomlike, the curtains fluttered in the uncertain light. Then he heard the shutters being cautiously pulled down. Again the impenetrable darkness of midnight surrounded him, but he sensed that a figure was moving toward him from the window.

Finally Barlach said, "There you are, Gulliver," and turned on his night lamp.

In the room stood a gigantic Jew in an old spotty and torn caftan, the red glow of the lamp falling on him.

The old man settled down again in his pillows. "I half

expected you to come tonight. I had an idea that you were an accomplished second-story man."

"You are my friend," said the intruder, "so I came." His head was bold and huge, his hands, noble, but everything was covered with terrible scars, bearing witness to inhuman tortures. Yet nothing had succeeded in destroying the majesty of this face and this human being. The giant stood motionless in the room, slightly bent, his hands on his thighs. His shadow played, ghostlike, on the walls and the curtains, his brilliant eyes rested with imperturbable clarity on the old man.

"How could you know that I found to be present in Bern necessary?" It came out of the beaten, almost lipless mouth, in an awkward, too careful mode of expression, as if from one at home in so many languages that he now does not immediately find his way around in German. However, his speech was without accent. "Gulliver leaves no trace," he said after a short silence. "I work invisibly."

"Everybody leaves a trace," replied the Commissioner. "I'll tell you yours: Whenever you're in Bern, Feitelbach, who hides you, puts an advertisement in the *Gazette* that he is selling old books and stamps. At such times Feitelbach has some money, I think."

The Jew laughed. "The great art of Commissar Barlach lies in discovering the obvious."

"Now you know your trace," said the old man. "And there is nothing worse than a criminologist who tells his secrets."

"I shall not cover my tracks for Commissar Barlach. Feitelbach is a poor Jew. He will never understand how to make money in business."

With these words the huge ghost sat down next to the bed. He reached into his caftan and pulled out a big dusty bottle and two little glasses. "Vodka," said the giant. "We shall drink together, Commissar; we have always drunk together."

Barlach sniffed the glass. He liked to drink at times, but he had a bad conscience. He thought to himself that Dr. Hungertobel would be rather taken aback were he to see all this: the liquor, the Jew, and the midnight, in which one should be asleep. "A fine patient!" Hungertobel would thunder and make a big fuss.

"Where did you get the vodka?" he asked after he had taken the first sip. "It's very good."

"From Russia." Gulliver laughed. "I brought it from the Soviets."

"Have you been in Russia again?"

"None of your business, Commissar."

"Commissioner," Barlach corrected him. "In Bern there are only commissioners. And not even in the Soviet paradise did you take off your awful caftan?"

"I am a Jew and I wear my caftan—as I have sworn. I like the traditional dress of my poor people."

"Give me another vodka," said Barlach. The Jew filled both glasses.

"I hope the cat-burgling was not too difficult,"

33

Barlach said with wrinkled brows. "Something illegal—what you've done tonight."

Gulliver answered shortly that it was important that he was not seen.

"But it is quite dark around eight o'clock and I'm sure they would have let you in. There are no police here."

"Then I may just as well climb the wall," replied the giant, and laughed. "It was childishly simple, Commissar. Up the wall and down a ledge."

"It's just as well that I'm being retired." Barlach shook his head. "I won't have to worry about you any more. I ought to have put you behind bars a long time ago. It would have been a catch all Europe would have appreciated."

"You won't do it because you know what I am fighting for," answered the Jew, unmoved.

"You really should get yourself some sort of papers," the old man suggested. "I don't think much of these rules and regulations myself, but for God's sake, there has to be some kind of order."

"I'm dead," said the Jew. "The Nazis shot me."

Barlach was silent. He knew what the giant was driving at. The light of the lamp surrounded the men with a quieting glow. From somewhere bells rang midnight. The Jew poured vodka. His eyes gleamed with a gaiety of a special kind.

"It was a beautiful day in May forty-five—we had the pleasantest weather, how well I remember a little

34

white cloud—when our friends from the Storm Troopers left me by accident in a miserable lime pit among fifty men of my people they had shot. And when after some hours I was able to crawl, covered with blood, under a lilac bush blooming not far away, the command that shoveled earth on top of the whole thing overlooked me. I swore then that from that moment I would lead the existence of a defiled and beaten animal—since it seems to suit God that we so often have to live like animals in this century. From then on I have lived in the darkness of graves, and stayed in cellars and the like. Only the night has seen my face, only the stars and the moon shone on this pitiful torn caftan. This is the way it should be. The Germans have killed me—I even saw my death certificate. My wife, an Aryan, had it—she is dead now, and she ought to be. She received it through the *Reichspost*. It was filled out neatly and was a credit to the good schools in which the German people are educated to civilization. Dead is dead, for Jews and Christians alike —excuse the order of enumeration, Commissar. For a dead man there are no papers and no borders, you have to admit that. He comes into every country where there are still persecuted and tortured Jews. *Prosit*, Commissar, I am drinking your health."

The two men emptied their glasses. The man in the caftan poured new vodka and said, as his eyes formed two sparkling slits: "What do you want from me, Commissar Barlach?"

35

"Commissioner," corrected the old man.

"Commissar," maintained the Jew.

"I want some information from you," said Barlach.

"Information." The giant laughed. "Reliable information is worth gold. Gulliver knows more than the police."

"We shall see. You were in all the concentration camps. You mentioned it to me once, though usually you don't talk much about those days."

The Jew filled the glasses. "At one time they considered me so terribly important that I was dragged from one hell to the next—and there were more than the nine of which Dante sings, who himself was in none. From each one I have brought the proper scars in this life after death that I lead." He held out his left hand. It was crippled.

"Maybe you knew an SS doctor named Nehle?" Barlach asked intently.

The Jew looked thoughtfully at the Commissioner for a while. "Do you mean the one from Stutthof?" he asked then.

"Yes."

The giant looked at the old man with a condescending smile. "He committed suicide on the tenth of August, nineteen forty-five, in Hamburg, in a run-down hotel," he said after a while.

Barlach thought—a little disappointed, The hell Gulliver knows more than the police! Aloud he said: "Did you in your career—or whatever one should call it—encounter Nehle?"

The Jew looked at the Commissioner searchingly, and his scar-covered face twisted into a grimace. "Why do you ask after this inhuman beast?" he retorted.

Barlach pondered how much he should tell, but decided to remain silent and to keep to himself the suspicion he had of Emmenberger.

"I saw his picture," he said accordingly, "and it interests me to know what became of someone like that. I'm a sick man, Gulliver, and I'll have to stay in bed a long time. One can't always read Molière, and so one lets one's thoughts wander. It occupies me to speculate about what kind of a human being a mass murderer is."

"All human beings are alike. Nehle was a human being. Consequently, Nehle was like all human beings. That is a treacherous syllogism, but a law we cannot alter," answered the giant, without taking his eyes off Barlach. Nothing in his mighty face betrayed his thoughts.

"I suppose you saw Nehle's picture in *Life*, Commissar," continued the Jew. "It's the only picture that exists of him. You could search this beautiful world forever and never find another. That's all the more annoying since the famous picture doesn't show much of this mystical torturer."

"Only one picture," Barlach said thoughtfully. "How so?"

"The devil takes better care of the select members

37

of his congregation than heaven does of its, and arranged the proper circumstances," the Jew replied sardonically. "Nehle's name was not in the membership list of the SS, displayed in Nuremberg for the use of criminology. His name is on no other list either—very likely he was not a member. The official reports from Stutthof to the SS headquarters never mention his name, and he was not carried in the personnel rosters. This man—who had so many victims on his quiet conscience—has an aura of legend and irregularity—as if even the Nazis were ashamed of him. And yet Nehle lived and nobody ever doubted his existence, not even hard-boiled atheists; for we all believe easily in a god that concocts the most hellish tortures. We used to talk about him in the concentration camps that were no better than Stutthof. But we talked of him as of a rumor, as of one of the meanest and cruelest angels in this paradise of judges and hangmen. And it remained that way, even after it was all over. From the camp itself nobody was left whom we could have questioned. Stutthof is near Danzig. The few inmates that survived the tortures were trampled to death by the Storm Troopers when the Russians came, who meted out justice to the guards and hung them. Nehle, however, was not among them, Commissar. He must have left the camp before."

"But they were looking for him," said Barlach.

The Jew laughed. "And for whom were they not

looking, Barlach? The whole German population had turned into a criminal affair. But nobody remembered Nehle, for there was nobody that could remember. His crimes would have remained unknown if *Life* hadn't carried the picture of a skillful and masterly operation, with the little flaw that it was executed without anesthesia. Humanity felt properly enraged, and so they started to look. Otherwise Nehle could have retired into private life, unmolested, to turn into a harmless country doctor —or the director of an expensive clinic."

"How did *Life* get the picture?" Barlach asked innocently.

"Very simple," the giant answered matter-of-factly, "I gave it to them."

Barlach shot up and stared, surprised, into the Jew's face. Gulliver does know more than the police, he thought, shaken. The adventurous life led by this shaggy giant to whom countless Jews owed their lives took place in areas where the trails of crimes and monstrous vices ran together. A judge with his own laws sat before Barlach, a judge who arbitrated according to his discretion, acquitted and condemned independent of the statutes and criminal codes of the glorious fatherlands of this earth.

"Let us drink vodka," said the Jew. "A drink is always good. You have to cling to alcohol, otherwise you might lose all sweet illusions on this Godforsaken planet."

39

And he filled the glasses and cried, "Long live humanity!" Then he poured down the drink and added, "But how? That is often quite difficult."

"You shouldn't cry out like that," said the Commissioner. "The night nurse will come. This is a decent hospital."

"Christianity, Christianity," said the Jew. "It produced good nurses and just as competent murderers."

For a moment the old man thought that he had had enough vodka, but finally he, too, drank.

The room spun around for a moment, Gulliver reminded him of a giant bat. Then the room stood still again, only it was a little bit crooked. But that he could take in his stride.

"You knew Nehle," said Barlach.

The giant replied, "I had dealings with him occasionally," and occupied himself with his vodka. Then he started to talk, but now no longer in his former cold, clear voice, but in a strangely singing tone, which became more marked when what he said was ironic or sarcastic, but which was sometimes nevertheless soft and tempered. And Barlach understood that everything, the wild and the sarcastic, was only the expression of an immeasurable sadness over the incomprehensible fall of a once beautiful world. And so it happened on that midnight that this gigantic Ahasuerus sat with him, the old Commissioner, lying desperately ill in his bed and listening to the words of this man of sorrows, whom the history of our epoch had made into a gloomy, frightening angel of death.

"It was in December of forty-four," said Gulliver in his sing-song, his pain spreading on its waves like a dark and oily spot, "and then in January of the next year, when the glassy sun of hope rose on the horizons from Stalingrad to Africa. And yet those were cursed moments, Commissar, and for the first time I swore by all our honorable scholars and their gray beards that I would not survive them. That I did, nevertheless, is due to Nehle, about whose life you are so eager to learn. Of this disciple of medicine I can report to you that he saved my life. He did it by throwing me into darkest hell and tearing me out by the roots of my hair, a method which, according to my knowledge, only one person survived, namely myself, who am damned to survive anything. And out of my colossal gratitude I did not hesitate to betray him by photographing him. In this perverse world there are good deeds one can only repay with villainies."

"I don't understand what you're trying to tell me," replied the Commissioner, who was not quite sure whether this was the vodka's fault or not.

The giant laughed and pulled a second bottle out of his caftan. "Forgive me," he said, "I'm making a long speech, but my tortures were even longer. What I want to tell you is simple—Nehle operated on me. Without anesthesia. This incredible honor was shown me. Forgive me again, Commissar, but I have to drink vodka and drink it like water when I think of it, for it was nasty."

"My God!" cried Barlach, and then again, into the silence of the hospital, "my God!" He was sitting up, and mechanically he offered his glass to the monster by his bedside.

"The story takes only a little nerve to hear, but far more than that to live through," continued the Jew in the old caftan in a singing tone. "One should finally forget these things, they say—and not just in Germany. Supposedly there are cruelties taking place in Russia, and sadists exist everywhere.

"But I do not want to forget anything, and not only because I am a Jew—the Germans have killed six million of my people, six million!—no, because I am still a human being, even though I live in my underground holes with the rats. I refuse to make a distinction between peoples and speak of good and bad nations; but a distinction between human beings I have to make. That was beaten into me, and from the first blow that cut into my flesh, I have distinguished between torturers and tortured. I don't deduct the new cruelties of new guards in different countries from the bill I present to the Nazis, I add them to it. I take the liberty of not distinguishing between those that torture. They all have the same eyes. If there is a God, Commissar, and my defiled heart hopes for nothing more, He will recognize not nations but only individuals, and

He will judge each one by the measure of his crimes and acquit each one by the measure of his own justice.

"Christian, Christian, listen to what a Jew has to say to you, whose people crucified your Saviour and who now has been crucified with his people by the Christians. There I rotted in the misery of my flesh and my soul in the Stutthof concentration camp, an extermination camp, as they called it, near the old proud city of Danzig, on whose account this criminal war had broken out. And no holds were barred there. Jehovah was far, occupied with other universes, or perhaps studying some theological problem that captivated his lofty spirit. And all the more wantonly his people were driven into death, gassed or shot as suited the Storm Troopers' whim and the weather conditions. With the east wind Jews were hanged and with the south wind dogs hunted down Judah.

"And then there was this Doctor Nehle, whose fate fascinates you so, you man of a well-mannered world. He was one of the doctors that grew like tumors in every camp. Blowflies who dedicated themselves with scientific eagerness to mass murder, who injected hundreds of inmates to death with air, phenol, acid, and whatever else was at their disposal between heaven and earth for this infernal entertainment. Or who performed their experiments on humans without anesthesia—out of sheer necessity, as they assured themselves, since the fat Reichsmarschall Goering had forbidden vivisections on animals.

Nehle was therefore not alone. Now I must speak of him.

"I have in the course of my travels through the various camps taken a close look at the torturers, and I know the types. Nehle was quite outstanding in his field. He did not participate in the brutalities of the others. I must admit that he helped the prisoners as much as this was possible—and as far as help could have a purpose in a camp the only purpose of which was extermination. He was terrifying in a different sense than the other doctors, Commissar. His experiments were not outstanding for their heightened torture. With the others, too, the skillfully chained Jews died bellowing under the knives, not due to the medical art but to the shock brought on by the pain. His devilry was that he did all this with the consent of his victims. As improbable as it sounds, Nehle operated only on Jews who volunteered, who knew exactly what awaited them and who even—this was his condition—had to watch other operations to see the full horror of the tortures before they could give their consent to suffer through the same thing."

"How was that possible?" asked Barlach breathlessly.

"Hope." The giant laughed, and his breast rose and sank. "Hope, Christian." His eyes gleamed with an abysmal, brutish ferocity. The scars in his face stood out prominently, his hands were like paws on Barlach's blanket. His broken mouth, that greedily sucked new

44

quantities of vodka into his tortured body, groaned in remote sadness: " '. . . Faith, hope, charity, these three,' as it says so nicely in the First Epistle to the Corinthians, thirteen. But hope is the toughest of them all, that is written into my, the Jew Gulliver's, flesh with red letters. Faith and charity, *they* went to the devil in Stutthof; but hope—that remained, and with it *you* went to the devil. Hope, hope! Nehle had it in his pocket, ready-made, and he offered it to everybody that wanted it—and many wanted it.

"It is incredible, Commissar, but hundreds had themselves operated on by Nehle—after they had stood, shaking and pale as death, and watched their predecessors die like dogs on the operating table and could still say No—and all of it for the mere hope of gaining the freedom Nehle promised. Freedom! How man must love it that he is willing to suffer anything to gain it! So much so that in Stutthof he went voluntarily into flaming hell, only to embrace the pitiful bastard of freedom offered to him there. Freedom is sometimes a whore and sometimes a saint, meaning something different to each person —to a worker something different than to a priest, to a banker something else, and to a poor Jew in an extermination camp like Auschwitz, Lublin, Maidanek, Natzweiler, and Stutthof, something else again! There freedom was everything that was outside the camp, but not God's beautiful world, oh no! In our unlimited modesty we hoped only to be brought back to such a pleasant place as Buchenwald or Dachau, which *now* represented golden freedom, where you ran no danger of being gassed, but only of being beaten to death. Where there was a thousandth of a thousandth of a hope of being saved by some improbable act of chance, against the absolute certainty of death in the extermination camps. My God, Commissar, let us fight for having freedom mean the same to everybody, so that nobody has to be ashamed of his kind of freedom. It is laughable. The hope of getting into a different concentration camp drove people in heaps to Nehle's flaying place. It is laughable" (and here the Jew actually broke out into a laugh of scorn, desperation, and rage).

"And I, too, Christian, lay down on the bloody trestle, saw Nehle's knives and pliers in the beam of the spotlight, shadowlike above me, and then sank into the infinitely graded range of pain, into those gleaming mirror-cases of torture! I too went to him in the hope of escaping once more, of getting out of this Godforsaken camp. For since this accomplished psychologist Nehle had proven himself helpful and dependable, we believed his promises, and you always believe in a miracle when the need is greatest. When I, the only one, survived a senseless stomach resection, he had me nursed back to health and sent me back to Buchenwald in the first days of February. But after endless journeying I was not destined to reach it. For there came, in the vicinity of the

46

town of Eisleben, that beautiful May Day with the blooming lilac bush under which I crawled.

"These are the deeds of the man sitting in front of you at your bedside, Commissar, his sufferings and his travels through the bloody nonsense of this era. And still the wreck of my body and my soul is drifting through the whirls of our time, which is devouring millions and millions, innocent and guilty alike. But now the second bottle of vodka is empty and it is necessary that Ahasuerus take the royal road across the window ledge and down the wall to the damp cellar in Feitelbach's house."

Gulliver had risen, and his shadow cast darkness in the room. But the old man did not let him go yet.

"What kind of a person was Nehle?" he asked, and his voice was hardly more than a whisper.

"Christian," said the Jew, who had hidden the bottles and the glasses again in his dirty caftan, "who can answer your question? Nehle is dead. He took his own life, his secret is with God who reigns over heaven and hell. And God does not share His secrets, not even with the theologians. It is deadly to investigate where there is only death. How often have I tried to sneak behind the mask of this doctor, with whom no conversation was possible, who spoke to none of the SS guards or the other doctors, let alone to an inmate! How often have I tried to penetrate what went on behind those glittering eyeglasses! What was a poor Jew like me to do if he never saw his torturer other than with a half-hidden face and in

47

a white coat? For the way in which I photographed him, endangering my life—nothing was more dangerous than to photograph in a concentration camp—was the way he appeared always. A bony figure, clad in white, slightly bent and silent, as if afraid to contaminate himself, he walked around those barracks with their gruesome want and misery. I believe he wanted to be cautious. Very likely he felt that one fine day the whole infernal apparition of concentration camps would disappear—to break out again from the depth of man's instincts like a pestilence with different torturers and different political systems. Through all this time he must have prepared his flight into private life—he was only temporarily employed in hell. According to this I calculated my blow, Commissar, and I aimed well. When the picture appeared in *Life*, Nehle killed himself. It was enough that the world knew his name, Commissar, for he who is cautious hides his name." These were the last words the old man heard from Gulliver. They were like the dull beat of a bronze bell, echoing terribly in the sick man's ear. "His name!"

Now the vodka took its effect. The sick man thought he saw the curtains over there by the window swell like the sails of a disappearing boat, heard the clatter of a shutter. Then, still less clear, a gigantic body dipped into the night.

But then, when the countless stars broke through the gaping wound of the open window, an unruly defiance rose in the old man, to survive in *this* world and to fight for a different, a better, one, to fight with this his pitiful body on which the cancer was gnawing, greedy and uncontrollable, a body that had been given another year, not more.

When the vodka started to burn in his intestines like fire, he began to bawl the "Berner March" drunkenly into the silence of the hospital, awakening the other patients. He could not think of anything stronger to sing. But when the disconcerted night nurse rushed in, he was already asleep.

THE SPECULATION

THE next morning Barlach awoke, as was to be expected, around twelve, shortly before lunch was served. His head was a little bit heavy, but otherwise he felt better than he had for a long time, and thought that every once in a while there was nothing like a good swig of schnapps, especially when you are bedridden and not supposed to drink. On his table was the mail; Lutz had sent the report on Nehle. Nowadays the organization of the police was really beyond reproach, particularly if you were going to retire, as was the case with him day after tomorrow, thank God. In Istanbul you had to wait for months for information. But before the old man could start reading, the nurse brought lunch. It was Nurse Lina, whom he liked extremely much, but she seemed rather cool, not at all as she had been. The Commissioner felt concerned. Somehow they must have found out about last night, he suspected. Incredible. Of course, it seemed to him as if he had sung the "Berner March" at the end, after Gulliver had left. But this must be a deception, he was not the least bit patriotic. Damn, he thought, if I could only remember.

The old man looked suspiciously around the room while he ate his oatmeal soup. (Always oatmeal soup!) On the table stood a few bottles and pills that had not been there before. Now what did that mean? The whole thing was not to be trusted. And furthermore, a different nurse appeared every ten minutes, to bring something, to look, to straighten something—one of them giggled out in the corridor, he heard it clearly. He did not dare ask after Hungertobel. It was quite all right with him that he would come toward evening. He had his practice in town during noon hours.

Gloomily the old man swallowed his thick grits with applesauce (this, too, was no variation), but was astonished when for dessert he got strong coffee with sugar—upon special order of Dr. Hungertobel, as the nurse explained reproachfully. That had never happened before. The coffee tasted good and made him feel gay. Then he dug into the dossier, which seemed the safest thing to do under the present circumstances.

But to his surprise Dr. Hungertobel entered the room shortly after one. His face was serious—as the old man ascertained with an unnoticeable movement of his eyes, otherwise seemingly absorbed in his papers.

"Hans," said Hungertobel, and resolutely stepped up

to the bed, "what on earth happened? I'm ready to swear —and with me every nurse in this place—that you were completely soused."

"Oh," said the old man, and looked up from his dossier. And then he said, "Well!"

"Yes," answered Hungertobel, "everything pointed to that. I tried in vain all morning to wake you up."

He was ever so sorry, regretted the Commissioner.

"It's practically impossible that you drank alcohol, unless you swallowed the bottle, too!" the doctor cried in desperation.

"I quite agree." The old man grinned.

Hungertobel admitted he was completely baffled, and polished his glasses. He always did that when he was excited.

"Dear Samuel," said the Commissioner. He readily admitted that it wasn't always easy to give shelter to a criminologist, and he, Barlach, would have to bear the suspicion of being a clandestine alcoholic. He would only like to ask him to call the clinic Sonnenstein in Zurich and to request a bed for Barlach under the name of Blaise Kramer. He should describe him as a freshly operated, bedridden, but rich patient.

"You want to go to Emmenberger?" Hungertobel asked, shocked, and sat down.

"Of course," answered Barlach.

"Hans," said Hungertobel, "I don't understand you. Nehle is dead."

53

"One Nehle is dead," corrected the old man. "Now we have to find out which one."

"For heaven's sake," cried the doctor in astonishment, "are there two Nehles?"

Barlach reached for his dossier. "Let us look at the case together," he continued calmly, "and examine whatever is striking. You will see, our art consists of some mathematics and a lot of imagination."

"I understand nothing," moaned Hungertobel. All morning long he had understood nothing.

"I am now reading the physical description," the Commissioner continued. "Tall, slim figure, gray hair, formerly brownish-red, eyes a greenish-gray, prominent ears, face slim and pale, bags under his eyes, teeth healthy. Special marks: scar on right eyebrow."

"That's him," said Hungertobel.

"Who?" asked the Commissioner.

"Emmenberger," replied the doctor. He had recognized him from the description.

"But this is the description of the dead Nehle in Hamburg, as set down in the police record."

"All the more natural that I mistook the man in the picture," Hungertobel said. "Anybody can resemble a murderer. My mistake has found the simplest solution in the world. Don't you agree?"

"That's one conclusion. But there are other conclusions that can be drawn. At first glance they may not seem as compelling; nevertheless, they will have to be examined as 'after all possible.' Another conclusion could be: It wasn't Emmenberger who was in Chile, but Nehle under his name, while Emmenberger was in Stutthof under Nehle's name."

"That seems a most unlikely conclusion," wondered Hungertobel.

"Of course," answered Barlach, "but a permissible one. We have to account for all possibilities."

"But for God's sake, where would that lead us?" protested the doctor. "So Emmenberger killed himself in Hamburg, and the doctor who is now directing the clinic is Nehle? Really!"

"Have you seen Emmenberger since his return from Chile?" the old man interrupted.

"Only a couple of times," Hungertobel answered, surprised at the question. He had finally put his glasses on again.

"You see, this possibility exists," the Commissioner continued. "There is another solution possible: the dead man in Hamburg was Nehle, returned from Chile, and Emmenberger returned from Stutthof, where he went under the name Nehle, to Switzerland."

"But you have to assume a crime," said Hungertobel, shaking his head, "in order to defend this odd theory."

"Right, Samuel," nodded the Commissioner. "We would have to assume that Nehle was killed by Emmenberger."

"With the same right we could assume the opposite:

Nehle killed Emmenberger. Apparently your imagination doesn't have the slightest inhibitions."

"This theory is also possible; it, too, we can accept, at least in the present state of our speculations."

"This is all nonsense," said the old doctor angrily.

"Possibly," Barlach answered stoically.

Hungertobel protested vigorously. The primitive manner in which the Commissioner was dealing with reality could easily be used to prove whatever one wanted to prove.

"A criminologist has the obligation to question reality," answered the old man. "That's the way it is. In this regard we have to proceed like philosophers, of whom they say that first they doubt everything. Then, of course, they dig into their wisdom and come up with the most beautiful speculations about the art of dying and life after death. Only quite likely we are even more useless than they. You and I have developed a number of hypotheses. All are possible. This is the first step. The second one will be to differentiate from the possible hypotheses the probable ones. The possible and the probable are not the same. So we have to examine the degree of probability in our theses. We have two people, two doctors: on the one hand Nehle, a criminal, and on the other, your former acquaintance, Emmenberger, the director of the clinic Sonnenstein in Zurich. We have two main hypotheses; both are possible. The degree of their probability is different at first glance. One hypothesis states that there is no connection between Emmenberger and Nehle, and is probable; the second one presupposes a connection and is improbable."

And that was what he had been saying all along, Hungertobel interrupted.

"Dear Samuel," answered Barlach, "unfortunately, I am a criminologist and obligated to find the criminal aspects of human relationships. The first hypothesis—the one that sets no connection between Nehle and Emmenberger, does not interest me. Nehle is dead and there is nothing on record against Emmenberger. But my profession forces me to examine more closely the second, improbable hypothesis. What is probable about it? It states that Nehle and Emmenberger exchanged roles, that Emmenberger, alias Nehle, was in Stutthof. Further, that Nehle, in Emmenberger's role, stayed in Chile and from there published articles in medical journals. Let's forget for the moment about the rest: Nehle's death in Hamburg and Emmenberger's residence in Zurich. We can admit quite openly that this hypothesis is fantastic.

"It is probable insofar as both Emmenberger and Nehle are doctors and resemble each other. Here is the point from which we can start. It is the first fact that appears in this jungle of possibilities and probabilities. Let's examine this fact. How do the two resemble each other? Resemblances occur often, great resemblances are rarer, and rarest of all are resemblances that correspond even in the accidental detail, in distinguishing marks that do not

57

stem from nature but from specific incidents. Here we have a case like that. Both of them not only have the same color hair and eyes, similar facial features and the same build and so on, but the same peculiar scar on their right eyebrows."

"Well, that's chance," said the doctor.

"Or skill," complemented the old man. Hungertobel had operated on Emmenberger's eyebrow. What was wrong with him?

"The scar came from an operation necessitated by a dangerously inflamed sinusitis," answered Hungertobel. "The cut is in the eyebrow to make the scar less visible. I really didn't do a good job on Emmenberger. It was partly bad luck—I usually operate quite skillfully. The scar became more prominent than was pardonable for a surgeon, and besides, part of his eyebrow was later missing," he said.

Was this operation frequent, the Commissioner wanted to know.

"Well, not exactly," answered Hungertobel. "Most people don't allow a sinusitis to progress to a point where one has to operate."

"You see!" said Barlach. "And the peculiarity of which I spoke lies in the following: this not-too-frequent operation was performed on Nehle; he, too, had part of his eyebrow missing, in the same spot—it says this in the police record. The corpse in Hamburg was carefully examined. Did Emmenberger have a scald mark on his lower left arm, about a hand wide?"

58

"What makes you ask?" Hungertobel was surprised. "Emmenberger once had an accident in a chemistry experiment."

"Because the corpse in Hamburg bore this scar," Barlach said, satisfied. He went on to ask if Emmenberger still had these scars today? It would be important to know —and Hungertobel had seen him.

"Last summer in Ascona," answered the doctor. "He still had both scars, I noticed it at once. Emmenberger was his same old self. He made a few spiteful remarks and otherwise hardly recognized me."

"Aha," said the Commissioner, "he hardly recognized you. You see, the similarity is so great that we no longer know who is who. Either we have to believe in a rare and strange kind of chance or a skillful trick. Probably the similarity between the two is not as great as we believe now. What appears as resemblance in passports and official papers is not sufficient to get the two mixed up. But when the similarity reaches such accidental things, the chances become greater that one can substitute for the other. The trick of a fake operation and an artificially induced accident would then have the purpose of changing mere similarity into identity. But we can only voice assumptions at this point in the investigation. However, you will have to admit that this kind of similarity makes our second hypothesis more probable."

"Is there no other picture of Nehle, aside from the one in *Life?*" asked Hungertobel.

"Three pictures from the Hamburg criminal police,"

answered the Commissioner. He took the pictures out of the folder and gave them to his friend. "They show a dead man."

"Not much left to recognize," said Hungertobel in a disappointed tone after a while. His voice shook. "A strong resemblance may exist, yes; I can imagine that Emmenberger might look like this in death. How did Nehle kill himself?"

The old man looked thoughtfully at the doctor who so helplessly sat by the bed in his white coat and had forgotten everything, Barlach's drunkenness and the waiting patients.

"With cyanide," the Commissioner answered finally. "Like most Nazis."

"In what way?"

"He bit on a capsule and swallowed its contents."

"On an empty stomach?"

"So they ascertained."

"Then it took effect immediately," said Hungertobel, "yet from the pictures it seems as if Nehle saw something horrible before his death." The two were silent.

Finally the Commissioner said, "Let's continue, even though Nehle's death may have its puzzles. We have to examine other suspicious points."

"I can't see how you can speak of further suspicious points," Hungertobel said, surprised and depressed at the same time. "That's rather exaggerated."

"Oh, no," said Barlach. "First of all, there is your experience as a student. I will touch on it only briefly. It helps me because it gives me a psychological clue as to *why* Emmenberger was possibly capable of the acts he committed *if* he was in Stutthof. But now I come to another, more important point: I am in the possession of the *curriculum vitae* of the man we know as Nehle. His background is grim. He was born in eighteen ninety, which makes him three years younger than Emmenberger. He is from Berlin. His father is unknown, his mother was a housekeeper who left the illegitimate child with the grandparents, led a vagabond life, wound up in a house of correction, and finally vanished. The grandfather worked with Borsig Corporation; himself illegitimate, he had come to Berlin from Bavaria in his youth. The grandmother was Polish. Nehle went to public school and entered the army at fourteen, was in the infantry for a year, and was then transferred into the medical corps as a sanitary orderly. This was done upon request of a medical officer. Here an irresistible desire for a medical career seems to have awakened in him. He was decorated with the Iron Cross for having successfully performed emergency operations. After the war, he worked as an attendant in mental and general hospitals, and prepared himself in his spare time for college-entrance examinations so that he could study medicine. But he flunked twice. He failed in Greek and Latin and in mathematics. Apparently the man was talented only for medicine. Then he became a nature-cure and miracle doctor with

61

a booming practice. He got into conflict with the law, and was punished with a not-too-great fine because, as the court stated, 'his medical knowledge is surprising.' People wrote petitions, the newspapers pleaded for him, but in vain. Then the noise about the case subsided. Since he kept getting into the same trouble again and again, the courts finally decided to 'overlook' his activities. In the thirties, Nehle doctored his way around Silesia, Westphalia, Bavaria, and Greater Hesse. Then, after twenty years, the big turning point—in nineteen thirty-eight he passes the examinations. (In thirty-seven Emmenberger emigrated from Germany to Chile!) His papers in Greek, Latin, and Mathematics were brilliant. The university passes a decree relieving him of the actual study and he receives his degree after again passing his examinations brilliantly. However, to everybody's surprise, he disappears into the concentration camps as camp doctor."

"My God," said Hungertobel. "What do you want to deduce from all this?"

"That's simple," answered Barlach, not without scorn. "Now let's look at the articles by Emmenberger which appeared in the *Swiss Medical Weekly*, and were written in Chile. They, too, are facts we cannot deny, and need to examine. These articles are claimed to be scientifically important. I believe that. But what I cannot believe is that they were written by a man who stood out for his literary style, as you claim Emmenberger did. One could hardly express oneself in a more awkward manner."

62

"A scientific treatise is no poem," protested the doctor. "After all, Kant wrote a rather complicated style."

"Leave Kant alone," grumbled the old man. "He wrote in a difficult manner, but not poorly. The author of these articles from Chile writes not only awkwardly, but ungrammatically. The man obviously never knew when to use the dative and when, the accusative. As you know, this has always been a characteristic of many Berliners. It is also strange that he often refers to Greek as Latin, as if he had not the slightest notion of either language; for instance, in Number Fifteen from the year forty-two, the word *gastrotomy*."

There was a deadly silence in the room.

For minutes.

Then Hungertobel lit a "Little Rose of Sumatra."

"In other words, you believe that Nehle wrote these articles?" he asked finally.

The Commissioner answered calmly that he thought it probable.

"I have nothing left to say," the doctor said grimly. "You proved the truth to me."

"We mustn't exaggerate now," said the old man, and closed the folder on his bed. "I have proven to you only the probability of my thesis. But probability still is not reality. If I say that it will probably rain tomorrow, it need not rain tomorrow. In this world, idea and reality are not identical. Otherwise it would be a lot easier, Samuel. Between idea and reality still lies the adventure of this existence, and we should in heaven's name leave it like that."

"It makes no sense." Hungertobel groaned and looked helplessly at his friend, who—motionless as always, hands behind his head—was lying in his bed. "You're running a horrible risk if your speculation is correct, for Emmenberger is then a monster."

"I know." The Commissioner nodded.

"It makes no sense," the doctor said once more, in a low voice, almost a whisper.

"Justice always makes sense," Barlach persisted in his undertaking. "Introduce me to Emmenberger. I want to go tomorrow."

"New Year's Eve!" Hungertobel was aghast.

"Yes," answered the old man. "New Year's Eve." And then his eyes gleamed ironically. "Did you bring me Emmenberger's treatise on astrology?"

"Of course," answered the doctor.

Barlach laughed. "Then give it to me. I'm curious to see whether it contains anything about *my* star. Maybe I have a chance after all."

ANOTHER VISIT

THE terrifying old man spent the rest of the afternoon painfully scribbling full a long sheet of paper and telephoning his bank and a notary. This idol-like, impenetrable sick man to whom the nurses came with more and more reluctance, spun his threads with unshakable calm, like a huge spider, unerringly fitting one conclusion to the next. In the evening, shortly after Hungertobel had informed him he could enter Sonnenstein on New Year's Eve, he received another visitor, of whom one could not know whether he came voluntarily or whether he had been summoned by the Commissioner. The visitor was a small, skinny fellow with a long neck. He wore an open raincoat, its pockets stuffed full of newspapers. Around his dirty neck wound a lemon-yellow spotty silk scarf. A beret was stuck on his bald head. The eyes flashed from underneath bushy brows; the strong hooked nose seemed much too big for the little man, and below it was a sunken mouth with no teeth. He was talking to himself, in verse form, it seemed, and, in between verses, separate words appeared like islands, *trolley bus, traffic police;* two things which seemed to irritate him beyond reason. His shabby clothes were in strange contrast to the elegant but old-fashioned black walking stick with a silver grip, which belonged to a different century and which he swung around in a wild fashion. At the main entrance he ran into a nurse, bowed, stammered a flowery excuse, got hopelessly lost in the maternity ward, nearly burst into the delivery room, filled with busy mothers-to-be, got chased away by a doctor, and tripped over one of the vases filled with carnations which stood in front of all the doors. Finally he was led into the new wing (they had caught him like a frightened animal). However, before he entered the old man's room, his walking stick got between his legs and he slid down the corridor and crashed against a door, behind which a very sick man was lying.

"These traffic policemen!" he cried when he at long last stood in front of Barlach's bed. (Thank God! thought the student nurse who had accompanied him.) "They are everywhere. A whole city full of traffic policemen."

"Except," answered the Commissioner, who felt it best to respond to the excited visitor, "that we need traffic police, you know, Fortschig. There must be law and order in traffic, otherwise even more people would get killed than there are already."

66

"Law and order in traffic!" Fortschig called with his squeaking voice. "All right, all right. But for that one does not need a special traffic police, for that one needs mostly more faith in the decency of people. All Bern has turned into one big traffic policemen's camp. No wonder that all pedestrians are going wild. But that's what Bern has always been—a desolate police village. A wretched tyranny has always nested in this city! Lessing wanted to write a tragedy about Bern when they told him of Henzi's pitiful death! Fifty years I have now lived in this hick town of a capital, and I won't describe to you what it means for a writer to vegetate and to starve in this sleepy, fat town. Terrible, simply terrible! For fifty years I closed my eyes when I walked through the streets—I did that even in my perambulator. I didn't want to see this unholy city in which my father rotted away. And now, when I open my eyes, what do I see? Traffic policemen, everywhere."

"Fortschig," said the old man, quite determined to interrupt, "we have other things to talk about than the traffic police," and he looked disapprovingly at the rundown, disreputable figure with big eyes like an owl, sitting in the chair and rocking pitifully back and forth.

"I really don't know what's the matter with you," the old man continued. "For God's sake, Fortschig, you are talented, you were a good fellow and the *Apfelschuss* you published was a good newspaper even though it was small. But now you fill its pages with indifferent junk about traffic police, trolley busses, dogs, stamp collectors,

67

ballpoint pens, radio programs, theater gossip, streetcar tickets, movie ads, senators, and restaurants. The energy and pathos with which you tear these things down—you always make everything sound like Schiller's *Wilhelm Tell*—is worthy of better things, heaven knows."

"Commissioner," cried the visitor, "Commissioner! Do not sin against a poet, a writer who has the infinite bad luck to have to live in Switzerland and, what is ten times worse, to live on Switzerland."

"Well, well." Barlach tried to appease; but Fortschig became wilder and wilder.

"Well, well," he screamed, and jumped off his chair, ran to the window and then to the door, and so on, like a pendulum. *"Well, well*—that's said so easily. What is excused by that *Well, well?* Nothing! By God, nothing! All right, I have become a ridiculous figure, almost one of those Theobalds, Eustaches, and Mustaches, or whatever they claim to be called—who fill the columns of our dear boring dailies with the adventures they have to endure with their collar buttons, wives, and razors—under a by-line, of course. But who did not fall to this level in this country, where they still make verses about the whispering of the soul when all around the world is crashing down about our ears! Commissioner, Commissioner, what *haven't* I tried in order to create a decent existence for myself with my typewriter. But I didn't even reach the income of a public charge. One attempt after the other had to be given up, one hope after another, the best dramas, the fieriest poetry, the most elevated stories! Houses of cards, nothing more! Switzerland made me into a fool, a whirligig, a Don Quixote who fights against windmills and herds of sheep. Here one is supposed to stand up for freedom and justice and all those other articles the fatherland has for sale, and to respect a society which forces one to lead the existence of a tramp and beggar if one dedicates oneself to the intellect instead of to business. They want to enjoy life, but not share one thousandth of this pleasure, not a penny! Once, in the thousand-year Reich, they uncocked their revolvers as soon as they heard the word *culture*—here they hide their purses."

"Fortschig," Barlach said sternly, "it's very good that you bring up Don Quixote—he happens to be one of my favorite subjects. We all ought to be Don Quixotes, if we have an open heart and a bit of brains under our skull. But it's not windmills we have to fight against like the shabby old knight in his tinny armor, my friend. We have to fight against dangerous giants, sometimes against monsters of brutality and shrewdness, and then again, against huge saurians with brains like sparrows. All of them monsters who exist, not in fairy tales or our fantasy, but in reality. That's our task, to fight against inhumanity in any form and under any circumstances. But it's important *how* we fight and that we do it a bit cleverly. The fight against evil must not be like a game with fire.

"But you, Fortschig, are playing with fire, because

you lead a worthy fight so foolishly, like a fireman who pours oil instead of water. If one reads the newspaper you publish, this pitiful little paper, one thinks at once all of Switzerland ought to be abolished. Much—very much—is not as it should be in this country, I can testify to that, and I lost quite a few hairs over it. But to throw everything into the fire, as if this were Sodom and Gomorrah, is wrong and indecent. You almost act as if you are ashamed to love this country still. I don't like that, Fortschig. One ought not to be ashamed of one's love, and love of one's country is still a good love—only it has to be stern and critical, otherwise it turns into blind partiality. And so one should start sweeping and scrubbing if one discovers dirty spots; but to tear the whole house down right away is senseless and ignorant. For it is difficult to build a new house in this poor hurt world. It takes more than a generation, and when it is finally built, it won't be better than the old one. It's important that one can tell the truth and that one can fight for it—without landing in jail. That's possible in Switzerland. We ought to acknowledge it and be thankful for it. We need not be afraid of senators and government councilors, or whatever their titles are. Admittedly, too many have to walk around in rags and try merely to survive from one day to the next. This is bad. But a true Don Quixote is proud of his poor armor. The fight against the stupidity and egotism of people has always been difficult and costly and brought with it neediness and humiliation. But it's a

70

holy struggle which must not be fought with wails but with dignity. You, however, thunder and curse into our Berners' ears what an unjust fate you are suffering among them and wish for the tail of a comet to sweep our old town away. Fortschig, Fortschig, you are subverting the battle with petty motives. You have to be above any suspicion of only being concerned about your bread-basket if you want to talk about justice. Leave off this talk about your own misery and the torn pants you have to wear, leave off this petty war about worthless things. God knows there are other things to fight in this world than the traffic police."

Fortschig's pitiful figure crawled back into the chair, and pulled up its little legs. The beret fell down, and the lemon-yellow scarf hung sadly on the little man's breast.

"Commissioner," he said in a whiny voice. "You are stern with me like Moses or Isaiah with the people of Israel, and I know how right you are. But for four days I haven't eaten anything warm and don't even have money to smoke."

Was he no longer eating with the Leibundguts, asked the old man, suddenly a little bit embarrassed.

"I had a fight with Mrs. Leibundgut about Goethe's *Faust*. She is for the second part and I am against it. So she did not ask me back. The second part of *Faust* was holy to his wife, Mr. Leibundgut wrote me, and he could no longer do anything for me," lamented the writer.

71

Barlach felt sorry for the poor wretch. He thought he had perhaps been too harsh with him, and finally asked grumblingly what on earth the wife of a chocolate firm president had to do with Goethe.

"Whom are they inviting now?" he finally demanded to know. "The tennis pro?"

"Botzinger, the musician," Fortschig answered meekly.

"Well, at least he has something decent to eat every third day for a few months," said the old man, feeling somewhat reconciled. "A good musician. Of course, nobody can listen to his compositions, not even I, and I am certainly used to terrible noises from my time in Istanbul. But that is beside the point. Anyway, I suppose he will soon disagree with Mrs. President about Beethoven's Ninth. And then she'll take the tennis pro back—they are much easier to dominate intellectually. I will recommend you to Grollbachs, the Grollbachs of the clothing store. They cook well, though a little bit on the greasy side. I think that may work out better. Grollbach is not literary and has no interest either in *Faust* or in Goethe."

"And the wife?" Fortschig asked, frightened.

"Stone deaf," the Commissioner calmed him. "A stroke of luck for you. And take that 'Little Rose' Doctor Hungertobel left, you may smoke it in here."

Ceremoniously Fortschig lit the cigar.

"Do you want to go to Paris for ten days?" the old man asked as if in passing.

"To Paris?" called the little man, and jumped off his chair. "Do I want to go to Paris? I, who worship French literature like nobody else? By the next train!" Fortschig gasped for breath in his surprise and excitement.

"My attorney Butz in the Bundesgasse has five hundred francs and a ticket," Barlach said calmly. "The trip will do you good. Paris is a beautiful city, the most beautiful city I know, aside from Istanbul. And the Frenchmen—I don't know, Fortschig, but the Frenchmen are still the nicest and most cultivated people. Not even a real Turk can hold a candle to them."

"To Paris, to Paris," stammered the poor devil.

"But first I need you for an affair that bothers me quite a bit," said Barlach, fixing his glance on the little man. "It's an unholy affair."

"A crime?" Fortschig was shaking.

"The point is to expose someone," answered the Commissioner.

Very slowly Fortschig put the "Little Rose" in the ash tray next to him. "Is it dangerous, what I will have to do?" he asked in a whisper.

"No," said the old man. "It's not dangerous. And in order to remove all possibility of danger, I'm sending you to Paris. But you must obey me. When will the next issue of your paper appear?"

"I don't know. When I have money."

"When could you send out an issue?" asked the Commissioner.

"At once," replied Fortschig.

Did he put out the *Apfelschuss* by himself, Barlach wanted to know.

"Alone. With a typewriter and an old duplicating machine," answered the editor.

"In how many copies?"

"In forty-five. It's a very small newspaper," came the whispered reply. "There were never more than fifteen subscriptions."

The Commissioner thought for a while. "The next edition of the *Apfelschuss* has to appear in a large number —three hundred copies. I'll pay for everything. I ask of you only that you write a certain article for it. What else the paper will carry is your business. This article (he handed him a big sheet of paper) will contain what I have written down here. But in your language, Fortschig, I want it in your language as in your best times. You need not know more than the information I am giving you, not even who the doctor is against whom this pamphlet is directed. My statements must not irritate you; they are true, take my word for it. In this article which you will send to certain hospitals will be only *one* lie, namely that you hold the proof of your statements in your hands and know the name of the doctor. That is the dangerous point. That is why you will have to go to Paris as soon as you have mailed the *Apfelschuss*. That same night."

"I will write and I will go," promised the writer, holding the sheet of paper the old man had given him. He looked completely different and was dancing around the room.

74

"You won't talk to a soul about your trip," commanded Barlach.

"Not to a soul. Not to a single solitary soul," swore Fortschig.

"How much will it cost for the three hundred copies?" asked the old man.

"Four hundred francs," demanded the little man, with shining eyes. He was proud to get into some money finally.

The Commissioner nodded "You may pick up the money from my good old Butz. If you hurry up, he will give it to you today. I've already talked to him on the phone. You will take off as soon as the edition is out," he ordered once more, filled by an invincible mistrust.

"At once," swore the little fellow, and raised his right hand. "That same night. To Paris."

But the old man was no calmer after Fortschig had left. The writer appeared more unreliable than ever before. He wondered whether or not to ask Lutz to have him guarded. Nonsense," he said then. "They retired me—I shall handle the Emmenberger case myself. Fortschig will write the article against Emmenberger, and since he will go away, there is no danger. Not even Hungertobel needs to know about it. I wish he would come now. I could use a 'Little Rose.' "

75

SECOND PART

THE ABYSS

WHEN the night set in on Friday—the last day of the year—the Commissioner reached the city of Zurich. Hungertobel was driving the car himself and, because he was worried about his friend, he drove even slower than he usually did. The city was illuminated by cascades of lights. Hungertobel got into droves of cars, gliding into the lights from all sides, disappearing into side streets and opening their intestines to let out men, women, all greedy for this night, for the end of the year, all ready to start a new one and to live on. The old man sat motionless in the back of the car, lost in the darkness of the small curved space. He asked Hungertobel not to take the most direct route. He stared at all this untiring activity.

Barlach held no great love for Zurich; he felt that four hundred thousand Swiss all in one place was overdoing it. He hated the main street they were driving along now. But during this sinister trip to an uncertain and threatening goal (this trip to reality, as he had said to Hungertobel), the city fascinated him.

Out of the black, dull sky it started to rain, then to snow, finally to rain again—silver threads in the lights. People, people! More and more masses pushed down on both sides of the street, behind the curtains of snow and rain. The trams were crowded, ghostlike faces became visible behind the windows, hands clutching newspapers, all fantastic in the silvery light, passing by, disappearing. For the first time since his illness Barlach felt like somebody whose time had passed, who had lost the struggle with death, the irrevocable struggle. The reason that irresistibly drove him to Zurich, this suspicion into which he had put so much of his energetic mind and yet which was merely a dream borne on the waves of his illness, seemed useless and worthless. Why should he fight? For what: To what purpose? He longed to give up, for an endless, dreamless sleep. Hungertobel cursed inwardly, he felt the resignation of the old man and reproached himself for not having put a stop to this undertaking. The uncertain nightly waves of the lake washed toward them, the car glided slowly across the bridge. A traffic policeman appeared, an automaton who mechanically moved arms and legs. Fleetingly Barlach thought of Fortschig, of the desolate Fortschig who now in Bern, in a dirty attic room, was feverishly writing the pamphlet. Then he lost this anchor, too. He leaned back and closed his eyes. The tiredness in him grew, became sinister and gigantic.

You will die, he thought. You will die one day, in a year, as the cities, the nations, and the continents will die one day. "Kick off," he thought, that's the word—"kick off"—and the earth will still revolve around the sun, in the same undiscernibly wavering course, rigid and without mercy, fast and yet so quiet, all the time, all the time. What does it matter whether this city here is alive or whether the gray, watery, lifeless plain covers it all—the houses, the towers, the lights, the people—was it the lead waves of the Dead Sea I saw shimmer through the darkness of rain and snow when we drove across the bridge?

He felt cold. The coldness of the universe, an ominous, large, stony coldness enveloped him for the fleeting trace of a second, for an eternity.

He opened his eyes and stared out again. The theater building appeared, was swallowed by the darkness. The old man looked at his friend in the front of the car. The calmness of the doctor, a benevolent calmness, did him good (he perceived nothing of Hungertobel's anxiety). Touched by the breath of the big Nothing, he became awake again and courageous. They turned left at the university, the road climbed, got darker, one curve followed another, and the old man drifted, keen, observant, and unerring.

THE DWARF

HUNGERTOBEL stopped in a park whose firs bordered on the forest, so Barlach assumed. For he could only guess at the edge of the forest against the horizon. Up here it snowed now in large clean flakes. Through the falling snow the old man glimpsed the front of the hospital. The car stood near the front entrance, which was set back into the wall and flanked by two carefully barred windows—from which one could watch the entrance, thought the Commissioner. Hungertobel lit a "Little Rose," without speaking a word, left the car, and disappeared into the entrance. The old man was alone. He leaned forward and scrutinized the building, as far as that was possible in the darkness. Sonnenstein, he thought, reality. The snow fell harder, none of the many windows was illuminated. Only once in a while a vague shimmer flickered through the white masses of snow. The white modern complex of buildings—mostly built of glass—lay before him like a cemetery. The old man became restless; Hungertobel did not seem to want to return. He looked at his watch—but hardly a minute had passed. I'm nervous, he thought, and leaned back, intending to close his eyes.

At that moment Barlach's glance fell through the car windows. The melting snow ran down in wide tracks, and he saw a figure hanging from the bars of the window to the left of the entrance. At first he thought he was seeing an ape, but then he recognized, surprised, that it was a dwarf, like one of those you sometimes find in a circus for the entertainment of the spectators. The little hands and feet were naked and gripped the bars as a monkey's would, while the huge head turned toward the Commissioner. It was a wrinkled stone-old face of a beastly ugliness, with deep cracks and creases, defiled by nature herself. It ogled at the old man with big dark eyes, motionless, like a weather-beaten mossy stone. The Commissioner bent forward and pressed his face against the wet window to see better, but the dwarf had already disappeared into the room with a catlike jump. The window was empty and dark. Now Hungertobel came, and behind him two nurses, looking all the more white in the incessant snowfall. The doctor opened the car door and was shocked to see Barlach's pale face.

"What's the matter?" he whispered.

"Nothing," the old man answered. "I just have to get used to this modern building. Reality is always a little bit different from what one expects."

84

Hungertobel sensed that the old man was not telling the truth and looked at him suspiciously. "Well," he replied, under his breath as before, "here we go."

Had he seen Emmenberger, whispered the Commissioner.

He had talked to him, reported Hungertobel. "There is no doubt possible, Hans, that it is he. I was not mistaken in Ascona."

The two were silent. The nurses waited, already impatient.

We are chasing a phantom, thought Hungertobel. Emmenberger is a harmless doctor and this hospital like any other one, only more expensive.

In the back of the car, in the now almost impenetrable shadow, sat the Commissioner, and he knew exactly what was on Hungertobel's mind.

"When will he examine me?" he asked.

"Now," replied Hungertobel.

The doctor felt how the old man perked up. "Then say good-by now, Samuel," said Barlach. "You're incapable of putting on an act and nobody must know that we are friends. Much will depend on this first interrogation."

"Interrogation?" wondered Hungertobel.

"What else?" answered the Commissioner in an ironic voice. "Emmenberger will examine me and I will interrogate him."

They shook hands.

The nurses came. Now there were four of them. The old man was lifted onto a stretcher of gleaming metal. Sinking back, he saw Hungertobel hand out the suitcase. Then the old man looked into the black, empty space from which the flakes fell softly in quiet, incomprehensible whirls, dancing, sinking, gleaming in the light, touching his face for a moment, wet and cold. The snow won't last long, he thought. The stretcher was pushed through the entrance, he heard Hungertobel's car drive off. He's leaving, he's leaving, he said quietly to himself. A white glittering ceiling curved above him, with large mirrors in which he saw himself, stretched out and helpless. The stretcher glided noiselessly through mysterious corridors; not even the steps of the nurses could be heard. Black numbers stuck to the gleaming walls on both sides; the doors were almost invisible, having been blended into the general white. In a corner shimmered the naked firm body of a statue. Again the soft and yet cruel world of a hospital surrounded Barlach.

And behind him the red fat face of a nurse, pushing the stretcher.

The old man had crossed his hands behind his neck.

"Is there a dwarf around here?" he asked in High German, for he had had Hungertobel describe him as a Swiss living abroad.

The nurse laughed. "But Mr. Kramer," she said, "what gives you such an idea?"

She spoke German with a Swiss accent, from which

86

he concluded that she was from Bern. He saw something positive in that, as much as her answer made him suspicious. At least he was among Berners.

And he asked, "What's your name, Nurse?"

"I am Nurse Clari."

"From Bern, aren't you?"

"Yes, Mr. Kramer."

I'll work on her, thought the Commissioner.

THE INTERROGATION

BARLACH, who was pushed into a room almost entirely of glass, opening with a blinding light in front of him, saw two figures, one of them slightly bent and slim, a gentleman even in his professional coat, with thickly rimmed glasses which nevertheless could not cover the scar on the right eyebrow. Dr. Fritz Emmenberger. The old man cast only a fleeting glance at the doctor for the time being. He occupied himself more with the woman, who stood next to the man he suspected. Women made him curious. He looked at her distrustfully. As a good Swiss citizen he found professional women somewhat uncanny. The woman was beautiful, he had to admit, and as an old bachelor he had a special weakness for that. She was a lady, he could tell that at first glance. In her white coat she stood, elegant and yet reserved, next to Emmenberger (who could, after all, be a mass murderer). But in Barlach's opinion she looked a little bit too noble.

You could very well put her on a pedestal, he thought bitterly.

"Greetings," he said, dropping the High German he had just spoken with Nurse Clari. He was happy to meet such a famous doctor.

"You are speaking Berner German," answered the doctor, also in dialect.

Living abroad did not mean he had to forget that, grumbled the old man.

Yes, so he could see, laughed Emmenberger.

Hungertobel is right, thought Barlach. He is not Nehle. A Berliner could never learn this dialect.

He looked at the lady again.

"My assistant, Doctor Marlok," the doctor introduced her.

"Well," said the old man dryly, glad to meet her. And then he asked abruptly, turning his head a little toward the doctor: "You were in Germany, weren't you, Dr. Emmenberger?"

"Years ago," answered the doctor. "I was there once, but mostly in Santiago de Chile," but nothing betrayed what he was thinking or whether the question bothered him.

"In Chile, in Chile," said the old man, and then once more, "in Chile, in Chile."

Emmenberger lit a cigarette and flipped a switch. The room was now in semidarkness, sparsely lit by the little blue lamp above the Commissioner. Only the operating table was visible and the faces of the two white figures in front or him; the old man recognized further that the room was closed off by a window through which broke a few distant lights. The red point of the cigarette, which Emmenberger was smoking, moved up and down.

Nobody smokes in rooms like these. The thought struck the Commissioner. I've already made him a little bit uneasy.

The doctor asked where Hungertobel was.

"I sent him away," replied Barlach. "I want you to examine me in his absence."

The doctor pushed up his eyeglasses. "I think that we can have faith in Doctor Hungertobel."

"Of course," answered Barlach.

"You're a sick man," Emmenberger continued. "The operation was dangerous and is not always successful. Hungertobel tells me that you are aware of this. That is good. We doctors need courageous patients, to whom we can tell the truth. But I would have welcomed Hungertobel's presence during the examination and I'm sorry to hear that he complied with your wishes. We doctors have to co-operate, that is a postulate of science."

As a colleague he could well understand that, answered the Commissioner.

Emmenberger was astonished. What did he mean? he asked. To his knowledge Mr. Kramer was not a doctor.

"That is simple." The old man laughed. "You hunt diseases and I hunt war criminals."

Emmenberger lit another cigarette. "Hardly a safe occupation for a private citizen," he said nonchalantly.

"Exactly," answered Barlach. "And now I've become ill in the midst of my hunt and come to you. I call that bad luck, to be here in Sonnenstein—or is it good luck?"

He could not yet give a prognosis, replied Emmenberger. Hungertobel did not seem terribly confident.

"But then you've not examined me yet," said the old man. "And that's the reason I didn't wish our good Doctor Hungertobel to be present. We must be unprejudiced if we want to make headway in a case. And we want to make headway, you and I, I think. There is nothing worse than forming an opinion about a criminal or a disease without studying the suspicious matter in its environment and observing its habits."

The doctor replied that he was right. It seemed logical to him, though he as a doctor understood nothing of criminology. Well, he hoped Mr. Kramer would recover somewhat from his profession here in Sonnenstein.

Then he lit a third cigarette and said, "I think the war criminals will leave you alone here."

Emmenberger's answer made the old man suspicious for a moment. Who is interrogating whom? he thought, and looked into Emmenberger's face. It appeared masklike in the light of the one lamp, with blinking glasses, the eyes behind them overly big and sarcastic.

"Dear doctor," he said, "you certainly don't want to maintain that there is no cancer in this country."

"Is that supposed to mean there *are* war criminals in Switzerland?" Emmenberger laughed, amused.

The old man scrutinized the doctor. "What happened in Germany, happens in every country if certain conditions occur. These conditions may differ. No person, no nation, is an exception. From a Jew, Doctor Emmenberger, who was operated on without anesthesia in a concentration camp, I learned that there is only one difference between human beings—that between torturers and tortured. But I believe there is also the difference between the tempted and the untouched. We Swiss, you and I, belong to the untouched. It is a blessing and not a mistake, as many say. For we are supposed to pray, 'Lead us not into temptation.' I came to Switzerland, not to look for war criminals in general, but to find a *particular* one, of whom I know no more than an obscure picture. But now I am sick, Doctor Emmenberger, and the hunt collapsed overnight, so that the hunted man does not even know how close I was on his track. A ridiculous spectacle."

Then he hardly had a chance left to find his man, the doctor answered indifferently, and blew out the cigarette smoke, which formed a fine milky-blue ring above the old man's head. Barlach saw how he gave a sign to the woman with his eyes. She handed him a syringe. Emmenberger disappeared for a moment into the darkness of the room; then, when he became visible again, he held a vial.

"Your chances are small," he said again, filling the syringe with a colorless liquid.

93

But the Commissioner contradicted him.

"I have yet another weapon," he said. "Let's take your method, Doctor. On this last dreary day of the year, after coming to your hospital through snow and rain, you receive me in the operating room for my first examination. Why do you do that? It's unusual to be so quickly whisked into a room which fills a patient with horror. You do it because you want to frighten me. You can only be my doctor if you control me, and I am a stubborn man—Hungertobel must have told you that. So you decided to give this demonstration. You want to dominate me in order to cure me, and fear is one of the means you have to utilize. It's the same in my dreadful profession. Our methods are alike. I have only fear left to utilize against the one I am looking for."

The syringe in Emmenberger's hand was pointing toward the old man. "You are a shrewd psychologist." The doctor laughed. "It's true, I did want to impress you with this room. Fear is a necessary means. But before I begin with *my* art, let's hear more about yours. How do you want to proceed? I'm curious. The hunted man does not know that you're hunting him, at least these are your own words."

"He senses it without being sure, and that's more dangerous for him," answered Barlach. "He knows that I'm in Switzerland and that I'm looking for a war criminal. He'll calm his fears and tell himself over and over that I'm looking for someone else, not him. For by means of a masterly trick he has escaped into Switzerland from

94

the world of unlimited crime, leaving his identity behind. A big secret! But in the darkest corner of his heart
he will sense that I'm looking for *him*, and nobody else,
only him—always. And he will feel fear, greater and
greater fear—the more improbable it seems to his in-
telligence that I am looking for him. And I, Doctor, am
in this hospital in bed, with my disease, my impotence."
He was silent.

Emmenberger looked at him strangely, almost with
pity. The syringe was in his hand.

"I doubt your success," he said matter-of-factly.
"But I wish you luck."

"His fear will kill him," answered the old man,
motionless.

Emmenberger slowly put the syringe on the little
table of glass and metal which stood next to the stretcher.
There it was, a vicious sharp thing. Emmenberger stood
slightly bent forward.

"Do you think so?" he said finally. "Do you think
so?" His eyes behind the glasses narrowed. "It's astonishing to find such a hopeful optimist in these times. Your
thoughts are bold; let's hope that reality will not let
you down one of these days. It would be sad if you
reached disheartening results." He said it softly, a little
bit surprised. Then he went slowly back into the darkness of the room. It became light again. The operating
room lay in a glaring light. Emmenberger stood next to
the light switches.

"I'll examine you later, Mr. Kramer," he said, and

smiled. "Your illness is serious. You know this. The suspicion has not been removed that your life is endangered. Unfortunately, this is my impression after our talk. Honesty deserves honesty. The examination will not be easy. It requires a certain amount of surgery. And we'd rather do that after New Year's, wouldn't we? One ought not to disrupt a beautiful holiday. The main thing is that I have you under my care now."

Barlach did not answer.

Emmenberger put out his cigarette. "For goodness sake, Doctor," he said to the woman, "here I am, smoking in the operating room. Mr. Kramer is an exciting visitor. You should call us both down, him and me."

"What are these?" asked the old man when the woman doctor handed him two reddish pills.

"Just a sedative," she said. But he drank the water she gave him with even greater misgivings.

"Call the nurse," ordered Emmenberger.

Nurse Clari appeared in the door. To the Commissioner she looked like a soulful hangman. Hangmen are always soulful, he thought.

"What room did you prepare for our Mr. Kramer?" asked Emmenberger.

"Number Seventy-two, Doctor Emmenberger," answered the nurse.

"Let's give him Room Fifteen," said Emmenberger. "We've better control over him there."

The tiredness that he had already felt in Hungertobel's car, overcame Barlach again.

When the nurse rolled the old man into the corridor, the stretcher made a sharp turn. Tearing himself out of his drowsiness, Barlach saw Emmenberger's face.

The doctor was observing him carefully, smiling and amused.

Gripped by a shivering fit, Barlach fell back.

THE ROOM

WHEN he woke up (it was still night, around ten-thirty; he must have slept about three hours, he thought), he found himself in a room which he regarded with surprise and not without concern. Yet he felt a certain satisfaction. He hated hospital rooms, and he liked the fact that this room bore more resemblance to a studio, a technical room, cold and impersonal, as far as he could tell by the blue shimmer of the night lamp burning at his left. The bed in which he was lying—in pajamas and well covered—was still the same stretcher on which he had been brought in. He recognized it at once, though with a few hand grips it had been changed into a bed. "They're practical here," said the old man into the stillness. He let the light from the revolving lamp fall into the room. A curtain appeared; behind it he suspected the window. It was embroidered with strange plants and animals. It's plain, I'm on a hunt, he said to himself.

He leaned back in the pillows and thought over what he had accomplished. It was little enough. He had followed through with his plan. Now it was necessary to continue, to spin the threads of his mesh tighter. It was necessary to act, but he did not know how to act and where to start. He pushed a button on the little table. Nurse Clari came in.

"Well, well, our nurse from Bern," the old man greeted her.

"Yes, Mr. Kramer, what is it? Finally awakened?" she said, her hands on her hips.

The old man looked at his wrist watch again. "It's only ten-thirty."

"Are you hungry?" she asked. "No? Shall I call the lady doctor? You've met her. She can give you another injection."

"Nonsense," growled the old man. "I haven't had an injection. Turn on the ceiling light. I want to look at this room. After all, one likes to know where one is."

He was quite angry.

A white, but not glaring, light shone. It was diffuse and one did not quite know where it came from. In this new light, the room was clear and sharp. Above the old man, the ceiling was a single big mirror. It annoyed him; it seemed sinister to have yourself over your head all the time. Mirrors everywhere, he thought, it could drive you crazy. He was secretly horrified by the skeleton that stared down at him whenever he looked up. That mirror lies, he thought. There are such mirrors that distort everything. I couldn't look that bony.

He looked around the room again, forgetting the nurse who waited, without moving. At his left was a wall made of glass against a gray background. Naked figures were carved into it, dancing men and women, linear and yet three-dimensional. From the right, grayish-green wall, between door and curtain, hung like a wing Rembrandt's "Anatomy," seemingly senseless and yet calculated, a combination that gave the room a somewhat frivolous air—all the more so since a black crude wooden cross hung over the door in which the nurse stood.

"Well, Nurse," he said, still surprised that the room had changed so much with the light. He had only noticed the curtains before, and had not seen the dancing men and women, the "Anatomy," and the cross. He was filled with the apprehension these unknown surroundings communicated. "Well, Nurse, this is a strange room for a hospital, a place that's supposed to make people well, not drive them insane."

"We're in Sonnenstein," answered Nurse Clari, and folded her hands across her stomach. "We comply with all wishes," she babbled on, gleaming with probity, "with the most pious ones and others. Really, if you don't like the 'Anatomy,' you can have the 'Birth of Venus' by Botticelli or a Picasso."

"Then I'd rather have 'Knight, Death and Devil,' "
said the Commissioner.

Nurse Clari pulled out a notebook. " 'Knight, Death
and Devil,' " she wrote down. "You'll have it tomorrrow.
A nice picture for a death chamber. I congratulate you.
The gentleman has good taste."

"I think," answered the old man, flabbergasted by
the crudeness of the nurse, "I think it hasn't gone that far
yet with me."

Nurse Clari slowly wagged her red fleshy head.
"Oh yes," she said firmly. "Only the dying are put here.
Exclusively. I've never seen anybody leave Ward Three.
And you *are* on Ward Three, that's all there is to it. We
all have to die sometime. Read what I've written about
it. It was published by Liechti in Waalkingen."

The nurse pulled out of her bosom a little pamphlet
and put it on the bed. *Clari Glauber: Death, Goal and
Purpose of Our Life. A practical guide.*

Should she get the doctor now? she asked tri-
umphantly.

"No," answered the Commissioner, still holding *The
Goal and Purpose of Our Life* in his hands. "I don't need
her. But pull the curtains and open the window."

The curtains were pulled aside, the light went out.
The old man turned out the night lamp, too.

The massive figure of Nurse Clari disappeared in the
rectangle of the door, but before it closed, he asked,
"Nurse! You answer all questions so openly, you'll

answer this one truthfully. Is there a dwarf in this house?"

"Of course"—it came brutally from the rectangle. "You saw him yourself, didn't you?"

Then the door closed.

Nonsense, he thought. *I* will leave Ward Three. Nothing to it. I'll call Hungertobel—I'm too sick to do anything against Emmenberger. Tomorrow I'll return to the Salem.

He was frightened and not ashamed to admit it.

Outside it was night, and around him was the bleakness of the room. The old man lay on his bed, hardly breathing.

The bells will have to start, he thought, the bells of Zurich, ringing in the New Year.

From somewhere a clock struck twelve.

The old man waited.

Again a clock struck from somewhere, then again—twelve merciless strokes. Stroke after stroke, like hammer blows on a gate of iron.

No bells, not even the distant cry of a happy crowd.

The New Year came in silence.

The world is dead, thought the Commissioner, and again and again, The world is dead. The world is dead.

On his forehead he felt cold sweat that slowly rolled down his temples. His eyes were wide open. He was lying motionless, resigned.

Once again he heard twelve distant strokes, fading

away over a desolate city. Then he felt as if he was sinking into a shoreless ocean, into an unknown gloom.

He woke up at dawn, in the twilight of the new day.

The room was more threatening than ever. For a long time he stared into the growing light, into the rising green-gray shadows, until he understood:

The window was barred.

DOCTOR MARLOK

"So he woke up," said a voice from the door to the Commissioner, who stared at the barred window. Into the room, which filled more and more with a foggy phantomlike morning, stepped an old woman in a white coat. Her features were wrinkled and bloated, and Barlach recognized only with difficulty and horror the face of the doctor he had seen with Emmenberger in the operating room. He stared at her, tired and shaken by disgust. Without paying any attention to the Commissioner, she pulled up her skirt and pushed a syringe through the stocking into her thigh. Then, after she had made the injection, she straightened up, pulled out a mirror, and applied make-up. Fascinated, the old man watched her. He did not seem to exist for this woman. Her features lost all vulgarity and once more gained the freshness and clarity he had noticed. Leaning motionless against the doorframe was now the woman whose beauty had struck him at the time of his arrival.

"I understand," said the old man, slowly awakening from his numbness, but still exhausted and confused. "Morphine."

"Certainly," she said. "One needs that in this world —Commissioner Barlach."

The old man stared into the morning. It grew darker, for now rain was pouring down outside into the snow which must still be there from the night. And then he said in a low voice, as if in passing: "You know who I am."

Then he stared outside again.

"We know who you are," said the doctor, still leaning against the door, both hands buried in the pockets of her white coat.

He asked her how they had found out, although actually he was not at all curious to know.

She threw a newspaper on the bed.

It was the *Bund*.

On the front page was his picture, as the old man noticed right away, a photograph taken in the spring when he still smoked Brazils, and the caption read: *The Commissioner of the City Police of Bern, Hans Barlach, retired.*

"Of course," muttered the Commissioner. Then, when he looked at it for a second time—angry and disconcerted—he saw the date.

It was the first time he lost his restraint.

"The date!" he screamed in a hoarse voice. "The date, Doctor! The date of the paper!"

"Well?" she asked, without a muscle moving in her face.

"It's the fifth of January," gasped the Commissioner desperately. Now he understood the absence of the New Year's bells this whole horrible past night.

"Did you expect a different date?" she asked in a sarcastic tone, obviously curious, lifting her eyebrows a bit.

He screamed, "What did you do to me?" and tried to sit up, but weakly fell back into the bed.

His arm flapped in the air a few more times, then he lay motionless again.

The doctor pulled out a cigarette case and took out a cigarette.

Nothing of all this seemed to touch her.

"I do not wish you to smoke in my room," Barlach said in a low voice but firmly.

"The window is barred," answered the doctor, and nodded with her head in the direction where the rain ran down behind the iron bars. "I don't think you have anything to say around here." Then she turned toward the old man and stood in front of his bed, her hands in the pockets of her coat.

"Insulin," she said, looking down at him. "The boss has given you an insulin treatment. His specialty." She laughed. "And you really want to arrest that man?"

"Emmenberger has murdered a German doctor named Nehle and operated without anesthesia," Barlach said cold-bloodedly. He felt that he had to win this woman over to his side. He was determined to risk every-thing.

"He has done much more, our doctor," replied the woman.

"You know it!"

"Of course."

"You admit that Emmenberger was camp doctor in Stutthof under the name of Nehle?" he asked feverishly.

"Of course."

"You admit Nehle's murder, too?"

"Why not?"

With one stroke Barlach saw his suspicion con-firmed, this monstrous, obtuse suspicion, built up from Hungertobel's reaction to an old photograph, the suspi-cion he had dragged around with him through these end-less days like a gigantic burden. Exhausted, he looked out the window. Small silvery drops of water rolled down the bars. He had longed for this moment of knowledge as for a moment of peace.

"If you know everything," he said, "then you, too, are guilty."

The woman looked at him with such a strange glance that her silence disturbed him. She pushed up her right sleeve. On her lower arm, deeply burned into the flesh, was a number, like a cattle brand. "Do I have to show you my back, too?" she asked.

"You were in a concentration camp?" Barlach cried, dumbfounded, and stared at her. He lifted himself pain-fully, resting on his right arm.

"Edith Marlok, inmate Four-four-six-six in extermination camp Stutthof near Danzig." Her voice was cold and dead.

The old man fell back into the pillows. He cursed his illness, his weakness, his helplessness.

"I was a Communist," she said, and pulled down the sleeve.

"And how could you survive the camp?"

"That's simple," she answered, and stood his gaze as indifferently as if nothing in this world could ever move her again, no human feelings and no human fate, be it ever so terrible.

"I became Emmenberger's mistress."

"But that's impossible." It escaped the Commissioner. She looked at him in astonishment.

"A torturer had mercy on a dying dog," she said finally. "Only a few of the women in Stutthof had the chance to become the mistress of an SS doctor. Any way of saving oneself is good. Aren't you trying everything possible to get out of here?"

Feverish and shaking, he tried for a third time to sit up.

"Are you still his mistress?"

"Of course. Why not?"

"But you can't be! Emmenberger is a monster!" Barlach screamed. "You were a Communist—you must have your convictions!"

"Yes, I had my convictions," she said calmly. "I was convinced that you must love this sad thing of stone and mud that revolves around the sun, this earth; that it's our duty to help humanity in the name of common sense to get rid of poverty and exploitation. My belief was no mere phrase. And when the house-painter with the ridiculous mustache and the silly curl on his forehead 'seized power,' the technically correct phrase for all the crimes he committed, I fled to the country in which I—like all Communists—had believed, to our all-mother, to the Soviet Union. Oh, I had my beliefs, and staked them against the world. I was determined like you, Commissioner, to fight against evil till the end of my unholy life."

"We must never give up this fight," replied Barlach softly, leaning back in the pillows and shaking with cold.

"May I ask you to look in the mirror above you?"

"I've already seen myself," he answered, anxiously avoiding a glance upward.

She laughed. "A beautiful skeleton grins at you— the Commissioner of the City of Bern. Our dogma of the struggle against evil which must never be given up, whatever the circumstances and the conditions, is correct in a vacuum or, what amounts to the same thing, behind a desk. But not on this planet on which we race through the universe like witches on a broom. My faith was great, so great that I did not despair when I was swallowed by the misery of the Russian masses, by the despair of that mighty land, which could be ennobled only by freedom of the spirit, not by violence. When the Russians buried me in their jails, without a hearing or a conviction, and

pushed me from one camp to the next without my knowing why, I did not doubt that this, too, had its place in
the grand scheme of history. When the splendid pact
came about, which Mr. Stalin closed with Mr. Hitler, I
saw its necessity, for was it not aimed at saving the great
Communist fatherland? But one morning, deep in the
winter of nineteen forty, after an endless journey from
Siberia in a cattle train, Russian soldiers drove me across
a miserable wooden bridge, in the midst of a crowd of
ragged figures. A dirty river lazily made its way underneath, carrying ice and wood. And on the other shore
the black figures of the Storm Troopers appeared
out of the morning mist. At that moment I understood
the betrayal, not only of us Godforsaken poor devils who
tottered toward Stutthof, but of the idea of Communism
itself, which only makes sense if it is one with the idea of
brotherly love and humanity. But now I have crossed
that bridge, Commissioner, I have crossed forever that
black, trembling bridge. I know now what human beings
are like. You can do anything with them, anything that
a tyrant or an Emmenberger ever thought of to give
them pleasure or to demonstrate their theories. You can
force any confession out of a man's mouth, for his will
is limited but the number of tortures is legion. 'Abandon
hope all ye who enter here.' I abandoned hope. It's
nonsense to fight and struggle for a better world. Man
himself wishes for his hell, prepares it in his mind and
brings it about by his deeds. It's the same everywhere,

there in Stutthof and here in Sonnenstein, the same gruesome melody, rising in sinister harmonies from the abyss
of the human soul. The camp near Danzig was the hell of
the Jews, the Christians, and the Communists. This hospital here, in the midst of the respectable city of Zurich,
is the hell of the rich."

"What do you mean by that? These are strange
words," said Barlach, listening fixedly to the doctor, who
fascinated and frightened him in equal measure.

"You're curious," she said, "and seem to be proud of
it. You dared to come into the lion's den from which
there is no escape. Don't count on me. Human beings
leave me indifferent, even Emmenberger who is my
lover."

THE HELL OF
THE RICH

SHE began talking again. "Why, for the sake of this lost world, Commissioner, were you not satisfied with your daily petty thefts? Why did you force your way in here, where there is nothing for you to seek? But I suppose a police dog that has served its time yearns for something 'higher.'" The doctor laughed.

"Injustice has to be sought where it can be found," answered the old man. "The law is the law."

"I see, you like mathematics," she replied, and lit another cigarette. She still stood by his bed, not hesitant and careful, as one approaches a sickbed, but as one stands next to a criminal who is already chained to a trestle and whose death one has recognized as necessary and desirable; a practical procedure which will extinguish a useless existence. "I thought from the first that you are the type of fool who swears by mathematics. The law is the law: x equals x. The most monstrous phrase ever to rise to the eternally bloody sky that hangs above us." She laughed again.

"As if there existed a destiny for man that is valid regardless of the amount of power he possesses. The law is not the law, but the power. This dogma is written down in the bloody valleys in which we were destroyed. Nothing is itself in this world, all is a lie. When we say *law*, we mean power; when we say *power*, we think of wealth; and when we say *wealth*, we hope to enjoy the vices of this world. The law is vice, the law is wealth, the law is the cannons, the trusts, the parties. Whatever we say, it is never illogical, except for the sentence that the law is the law, which alone is a lie. Mathematics lies, common sense, intellect, the arts—they all lie.

"What do you want, Commissioner? We are born on some brittle clod, without being asked, without knowing why. We stare into a universe, into gigantic emptiness and plenty, a senseless waste—and so we drift to the distant cataracts which we will have to encounter—the only thing of which we are certain. We live in order to die, we breathe and talk, we love and have children and grandchildren. And together with them, whom we love and bore, we are turned into carcasses, to disintegrate into the indifferent, dead elements of which we are composed. The cards were mixed, dealt, and gathered together; *c'est ça*. We have nothing else but this drifting piece of dirt and ice to which we cling. And so we wish that this our only life—this fleeting moment in the face of the rainbow that spans the abyss of foam and steam—should be a happy one. We wish the plenty of the earth to be ours for the short time that she carries us, she who is the only mercy bestowed upon us. But this is not so and will never be. And the crime, Commissioner, is not that it is not so, that there is poverty and misery, but that there are rich *and* poor, that the ship with which we all sink still has cabins for the powerful and rich next to the mass quarters of the poor.

"We all have to die, they say, so it does not matter. Dying is dying. Oh, this farcical logic! The dying of the poor is one thing and the dying of the rich and mighty, another. There are worlds between the bloody tragicomedy of the weak and that of the powerful. The poor man dies in the same way in which he lived—on a sack in a cellar, on a torn mattress, or on the bloody field of honor. But the rich man dies differently. He has lived in luxury and wants to die in luxury. He is cultivated and applauds his own departure. Bravo, my friends, the performance is over! Life was a farce, dying a phrase, the funeral an advertisement, and the whole thing a business deal. *C'est ça.*

"If I could show you through this hospital, Commissioner, which has made me what I am, neither man nor woman, only flesh that needs always bigger doses of morphine to make the jokes about this world it deserves

—I'd show you *how* the rich die. I'd unlock the fantastic sickrooms for you, the gaudy, cunning rooms in which they rot, the gleaming cells of lust and torture, caprice and crime."

Barlach did not answer. He lay there, sick and motionless, his face turned away. The woman bent over him.

"I'd tell you," she continued without mercy, "the names of those who've died here, and *are* dying here—the politicians, bankers, industrialists, the mistresses, and the widows—all with famous names. And those unknown criminals who with one big deal that costs them nothing earn the millions that cost us everything. They die here in this hospital. Sometimes they make blasphemous jokes about their rotting bodies, sometimes they rear up and utter wild curses against their fate, that they have so much and yet must die. Sometimes they blubber the most disgusting prayers in their brocade-and-silk-filled rooms, prayers that they may not have to exchange the bliss up here for the bliss of paradise. Emmenberger grants them everything and greedily they take everything he offers. But they need more, they need hope. This, too, he grants them. But the trust they place in him is trust in the devil, and the hope he gives them is hell. They have left God and found a new god. Voluntarily these sick people undergo tortures, so that they may live a few days, a few minutes more, so that they will not be snatched away from the things they love more than heaven and hell, more than salvation and damnation—their power and the earth which gave them this power. Here, too, the boss operates without anesthesia. Everything Emmenberger did in Stutthof, he does here, in the middle of Switzerland, in the middle of Zurich, unmolested by the police and the laws of this country. Yes, he even does it in the name of science and humanity. Unerringly he gives what people want of him—tortures, nothing but tortures."

"No!" screamed Barlach. "No! He must be destroyed!"

"Then mankind must be destroyed," she answered.

Again he screamed his hoarse, desperate *no* and painfully sat up.

"No, no," it came out of his mouth, but he could only whisper.

Indifferently, the doctor pushed his shoulder, and he fell back helplessly.

"No, no!" he groaned from the pillows.

"You fool." She laughed. "What do you want with your *no, no?* in the black mining town from which I came, I, too, said my *no, no* to this world full of misery and exploitation, and I began to work. In the Party, in evening courses, in the university, and more and more determinedly in the Party. I studied and worked for my *no, no.* But now, Commissioner, now standing next to you in my white coat on this misty morning of rain and snow, I know that this *no, no* has become senseless. The world is too old to become a *yes, yes.* Good and bad were too tightly intertwined on the night of that Godforsaken

117

wedding between heaven and hell which produced mankind ever to be separated again, ever to permit such statements as, 'This is well done and that is evil; this will lead to good and that, to bad.' Too late! We no longer know what we are doing, what actions will result from our obedience or our rebellion, what exploitation, what crime sticks to the fruit we eat, to the bread and milk we give our children. We kill without seeing the victim, without the murderer knowing it. Too late!

"The temptation of this existence was too great and the human being, too small for the mercy which consists of living and not being Nothing. Now we are deadly ill, eaten by the cancer of our deeds. The world is foul, Commissioner, rotting like a badly stored fruit. What do we still want! The infernal stream of lava we conjured up in the days of our victories, our fame, and our wealth, the stream which now lights our night, can no longer be restricted to the tunnels through which it rose. Only in our dreams can we win back what we have lost, in the burning pictures of ardent longing morphine gives us. So I, Edith Marlok, commit the crimes demanded of me for the colorless liquid I inject under my skin, which bestows upon me during the day the courage to jeer and during the night my dreams, so that I possess in a fleeting illusion what no longer exists—the world as God created it. Emmenberger, your compatriot, knows people and knows what they are useful for. He puts his merciless levers where we are weakest, in the deadly consciousness of our eternal damnation."

"Go," he whispered. "Go now!"

The doctor laughed. Then she stood up, beautiful, proud, distant.

"You want to fight evil and are afraid of my *c'est ça*," she said, putting on make-up again, leaning on the door with its senseless and lonely old wooden cross. "You shudder already before a low and defiled servant of this world. How will you stand up to him, the Prince of Hell himself, Emmenberger?"

And then she threw a newspaper and a brown envelope on his bed.

"Read your mail, sir. I've a feeling you'll be surprised at what you accomplished with your good will."

KNIGHT, DEATH

AND DEVIL

AFTER the doctor had left the old man, he stayed motionless for a long time. His suspicion had been confirmed, but what should have given him satisfaction only filled him with horror. He sensed that he had calculated correctly but acted foolishly. Only too well he recognized the helplessness of his body. He had lost six days, six dreadful days of which he knew nothing. Emmenberger knew who was after him and had attacked.

Then, finally, when Nurse Clari came with coffee and rolls, he sat up and ate, suspicious but obstinate, determined to overcome his weakness and to counter-attack.

"Nurse Clari," he said, "I'm from the police. Maybe it's better we talk openly with each other."

"I know, Commissioner Barlach," answered the nurse, threatening and huge next to his bed.

"You know my name and are therefore informed," Barlach continued. He was puzzled. "Do you know, too, why I'm here?"

"You want to arrest our boss," she said, looking down at him.

"Yes, the boss." The Commissioner nodded. "And do you know that your boss killed many people in the Stutthof concentration camp in Germany?"

"My boss has been converted," Nurse Clari Glauber from Bern answered proudly. "His sins are forgiven."

"How so?" Barlach asked, flabbergasted, staring at this monster of probity that stood by his bed, her hands folded over her stomach, beaming and convinced.

"He read my brochure," she said.

"The Goal and Purpose of Our Life?"

"That's right."

But that was nonsense, the sick man cried angrily. Emmenberger was still killing people.

"Before he killed out of hatred, now out of love," the nurse replied gaily. "He kills as a doctor, because people secretly long for death. Just read my brochure. Man must go through death to his higher possibilities."

"Emmenberger is a criminal," gasped the Commissioner, helpless in the face of such bigotry. These goddamned sectarians, he thought desperately.

"The meaning and purpose of our life cannot be a crime." Nurse Clari shook her head disapprovingly and cleared away the dishes.

"I'll turn you over to the police as an accomplice,"

122

threatened the Commissioner, reaching for his cheapest weapon, as he well knew.

"You're on Ward Three," said Nurse Clari, sad over this stubborn man, and walked out.

Angrily the old man reached for the mail. He recognized the envelope. It was one of those in which Fortschig usually mailed out his *Apfelschuss*. He opened it, and the newspaper fell out. It had been written, as always during the last twenty-five years, with a rusty, rattling typewriter, with a bad *l* and *r*. "*Der Apfelschuss*, Swiss Protestpaper for the Inland and Surroundings, published by Ulrich Friedrich Fortschig," was the printed title, and underneath, typed with the typewriter:

SS Torturer as Clinic Director

"If I did not have the evidence [wrote Fortschig], this terrible, clear, and irrefutable evidence, that neither a criminologist nor a poet but reality alone can conjure up, I would be forced to describe as the diabolical scheme of a pathological fantasy what truth now forces me to write down.

"Truth shall have the floor—even if it makes us turn pale, even if it forever shakes the trust we put—to this day and in spite of everything—in mankind. That a human being, a Berner, under a strange name, went about his bloody trade in an extermination camp near Danzig— I dare not describe in more detail with what bestiality— horrifies us. But that he can direct a clinic in Switzerland is a disgrace for which we can find no words and an indication that we, too, are reaching the end of the road. May these words initiate legal action, which—though terrible and embarrassing for our country—has to be undertaken. For our honor is at stake, and the harmless rumor that we are struggling honestly through the jungle of these times (though we sometimes earn rather a lot of money with watches, cheese, and a few not-so-important weapons).

"In this spirit I shall take action. We will lose everything if we gamble with justice. Justice must not be toyed with! This criminal however, a doctor in Zurich whom we shall not pardon, for he never pardoned, whom we blackmail, for he blackmailed, and whom we will finally kill, for he killed countless numbers—we know it is a death sentence we are writing down for him [Barlach had to read this sentence twice]. That director of a private clinic—to be blunt—is asked to give himself up to the Zurich criminal police. Mankind, which is capable of everything and which in an even higher degree understands murder as it understands no other art, this mankind of which we here in Switzerland are part—for we carry the same seeds of the misfortune, the same tendency to regard morality as unremunerative and the remunerative as moral—should finally learn from the example of this beast of a mass murderer that the sadly disregarded force of the spirit breaks open even closed mouths and has them bring about their own destruction."

As much as this bombastic text complied with Barlach's original plan, which quite simply had been intended to frighten Emmenberger (the rest would somehow follow, he had thought, with the negligent self-confidence of an old criminologist), he realized now clearly that he had made a mistake. The doctor could certainly not be regarded as a man who allowed himself to be threatened. Fortschig's life was in danger, sensed the Commissioner, but he hoped that the writer was already in Paris and therefore safe.

Then, unexpectedly, there seemed to be a possibility for Barlach to establish contact with the outside world.

A workman had entered the room, an enlarged reproduction of Dürer's "Knight, Death and Devil" under his arm. The Commissioner looked at the man. He seemed to be a good-natured though slightly run-down–looking person of about fifty years, clad in blue overalls. He immediately began to take down the "Anatomy."

"Hey," called the Commissioner. "Come over here." The man continued with his work. Once he dropped a pair of pliers, then a screwdriver, and bent down awkwardly to pick them up.

"You!" Barlach called impatiently, since the workman paid not the slightest attention to him. "I'm Police Commissioner Barlach. Do you understand? My life is in danger. Leave this house after you have finished your work and contact Inspector Lutz—every child will tell you how. Or go to any police station and have them call Lutz. Do you understand? I need this man. He must come at once."

The laborer still paid no attention to the old man,

who painfully formulated the words—more and more he had difficulty speaking. The "Anatomy" was taken down and now the man examined the Dürer, first from close up, then holding it away from himself with both arms. Through the window fell a milky light. For a moment it seemed to the old man that he could spot a lusterless ball swimming behind the white fog. It had stopped raining. The workman shook his head a few times; the painting seemed to frighten him. He turned to Barlach and said in a strange, too clearly formulated manner, very slowly: "There is no devil."

"Yes!" screamed Barlach hoarsely. "There is a devil! Here in this hospital. Why don't you listen! They probably told you I'm crazy and babble nonsense, but my life is in danger, don't you understand?—my life is in danger. That's the truth, man, the truth, nothing but the truth!"

The workman had put up the painting now and turned to Barlach. He grinned and pointed to the knight who sat so motionless on his horse. He made a few inarticulate, gurgling sounds which Barlach did not understand right away, but which finally made sense: "Knight *kaputt*"—it came slowly and clearly out of the twisted mouth of the man with the blue overalls—"knight *kaputt*, knight *kaputt!*"

Only after he had left the room and clumsily slammed the door did the old man understand that he had talked to a deaf-mute.

He reached for the newspaper. It was the *Berner Bund* he unfolded.

Fortschig's face was the first thing he saw, and the caption read: ULRICH FRIEDRICH FORTSCHIG, and next to it—a cross.

FORTSCHIG ✠

"The unhappy existence of the more infamous than famous writer Fortschig came to an end during Tuesday night in a manner as yet unclear," read Barlach, who felt as if he was being choked. "This man," continued the unctuous reporter of the *Berner Bund*, "upon whom nature bestowed such beautiful talents, did not understand how to make the most of his gifts. He began [the article continued] with expressionistic plays which created a stir among the boulevard literati. But he was less and less capable of giving form to his creative powers [But at least they were creative powers, the old man thought, in a bitter mood]. Finally he succumbed to the unfortunate idea of publishing his own newspaper, which appeared irregularly enough in editions of about fifty typewritten copies. All those who ever saw the content of this example of the gutter press know enough. It consisted of attacks directed not only against everything that is holy to us but against well-known and generally esteemed personalities as well. He sank lower and lower, and was often seen completely drunk, staggering from one inn to the next, with his famous yellow scarf—he was nicknamed Lemon throughout the city—accompanied by a few students who celebrated him as a genius.

"About his death the following is known. Since New

Year's Fortschig has been continually drunk. Financed by some good-natured private source, he had published his *Apfelschuss* once more. It was a particularly sad piece of work, containing an attack against an unnamed, very likely nonexistent doctor, for the sole purpose of creating a scandal. The attack, by the way, has been rejected as absurd by the members of the Medical Association. An indication of just how much of this article was pure fantasy is to be seen in the fact that Fortschig blabbered to one and all about his intention of spending ten days in Paris—while at the same time the article demanded with a great deal of pathos that the unknown doctor give himself up to the Zurich police.

"However, he was not destined to reach Paris. He had already put off his journey by one day, and on Tuesday evening, gave a dinner in his shabby apartment. He had invited the musician Botzinger and the students Fiedling and Sturler. Around four o'clock in the morning, Fortschig—who was very drunk—went into the bathroom, which is situated across the corridor from his room. He left the door to his study open, to clear the air of tobacco smoke. The door of the bathroom was therefore visible to his companions, who continued to feast at the table without noticing anything unusual. When he had not returned after half an hour, they grew concerned and, since there was no answer to their calling and knocking, they rattled the locked door, but were unable to open it. Finally they called the policeman Gerber and the nightwatchman Brenneisen, who broke the door down. The unfortunate writer was crumpled on the floor—dead.

"Nobody knows how the tragedy occurred. However, there is no question of a crime, as the Chief of Police, Dr. Lutz, informed the press in today's interview. Though the investigation pointed to some hard object having hit Fortschig from above, the physical layout makes this impossible. The light shaft into which the window opens (the bathroom is on the top floor) is narrow, and it would be impossible for a person to climb up or down there. Appropriate experiments by the police proved this beyond doubt. Furthermore, the door was locked from the inside, and the well-known tricks by which this can be feigned are out of the question. The door has no key-hole and is closed by means of a heavy bolt. No other explanation remains than that the writer took an unfortunate tumble, all the more possible since he was—as has been established—intoxicated to the point of senselessness."

As soon as the old man had read this, he dropped the newspaper. His hand clutched the blanket.

"The dwarf! The dwarf!" he screamed into the room, for all at once he had understood how Fortschig had met his death.

"Yes, the dwarf," answered a quiet, deliberate voice from the door, which had opened without his noticing it.

"You'll admit, Commissioner, that I've availed myself of an executioner whom it will hardly be easy to find."

In the door stood Emmenberger.

THE CLOCK

THE doctor closed the door.

He was not in a white coat, as the Commissioner had first seen him, but in a dark striped suit with a white tie on a silver-gray shirt, a careful appearance, almost flashy, all the more so since he wore heavy yellow gloves, as if he was afraid to soil himself.

"So now we Berners are among ourselves," said Emmenberger, and made a slight, more polite than ironical, obeisance toward the helpless skeleton that was Barlach. Then he took a chair from behind the curtain and sat down next to the old man's bed, turning the back of the chair toward the Commissioner so that he could press it against his chest and put his arms on it.

The old man had regained his composure.

"You had the poor devil killed," said Barlach.

"It seems to me that if someone writes a death sentence with so much pathos, he needs his ears boxed," the other answered in an equally matter-of-fact voice. "Even writing has become a dangerous profession today, which can only further it."

"What do you want from me?" asked the Commissioner.

Emmenberger laughed. "Is it not rather up to me to ask what you want from me?"

"You know that perfectly well," replied the Commissioner.

"Of course," answered the doctor. "I know that perfectly well. And so you know perfectly well what I want from you."

Emmenberger stood up and walked to the wall, looking at it for a moment, his back toward the Commissioner. Somewhere he must have pushed a button or a lever, for the wall with the dancing men and women opened noiselessly, like a folding door. Behind it, a wide room became visible, with glass cupboards containing surgical instruments, gleaming knives and scissors in metal containers; bottles and a thin red leather mask—all spotless and all neatly arranged. In the middle of the room stood an operating table. At the same time—slowly and threateningly—a heavy metal screen lowered itself across the window panes. The room lit up. The old man noticed for the first time that neon tubes had been fitted into the ceiling, between the mirrors. Above the cupboards hung in the blue light a big, round, greenish, gleaming disk—a clock.

132

"You intend to operate on me without anesthesia," whispered the old man.

Emmenberger did not answer.

"Since I am an old weak man, I am afraid I will scream," the Commissioner continued. "I do not believe that you will find me a brave victim."

This, too, Emmenberger did not answer.

"Do you see the clock?" he asked instead.

"I do," said Barlach.

"It is now ten-thirty," said the other man, and compared it with his wrist watch. "I will operate on you at seven o'clock."

"In eight and a half hours."

"In eight and a half hours," confirmed the doctor. "But now we still have to talk about something else, I think, my friend. We cannot avoid it; then I won't disturb you any more. They say one likes to be alone with oneself for the last hours. All right. But you are creating an inordinate amount of trouble for me." He sat down on the chair again, its back pressed against his chest.

"I thought you were used to that," replied the old man.

For a moment Emmenberger was startled. "I'm glad," he said finally, shaking his head, "that you've not lost your sense of humor. First of all, there is Fortschig. He was condemned to death and executed. My dwarf did good work. It was not easy for Tom Thumb to climb up the light shaft—after a strenuous promenade across the wet roofs, surrounded by purring cats—and to strike such a really energetic and fatal blow with my keys. I was actually curious, as I waited for the little monkey in my car next to the Jewish cemetery, whether he could do it. But such a devil, hardly three and a half feet high, works noiselessly and, most important, invisibly. Two hours later he came hopping along in the shadow of the trees. You, Commissioner, I will have to take on myself. That won't be difficult. But let us spare ourselves conversation which could only be painful for you. But what, in the name of heaven, shall we do with our mutual acquaintance, with our dear old friend Doctor Samuel Hungertobel?"

"What makes you think of him?" asked the old man guardedly.

"He brought you here."

"I have nothing to do with him," the Commissioner said quickly.

"He telephones twice a day and asks how his old friend Mr. Kramer is coming along and wants to talk to you," Emmenberger said. He seemed grieved.

Involuntarily, Barlach looked at the clock over the cupboards.

"Yes, it's a quarter to eleven," said the doctor, and regarded the old man in a thoughtful, but not hostile, manner. "Let's get back to Hungertobel."

"He was kind to me, tried to help me get well, but he has nothing to do with us two," the Commissioner replied stubbornly.

"Did you read the article under your picture in the *Bund?*"

Barlach thought for a moment, trying to figure out what Emmenberger was driving at with this question.

"I don't read newspapers."

"It stated that in you a famous local personality had retired," said Emmenberger, "and yet Hungertobel admitted you here under the name of Blaise Kramer."

The Commissioner revealed nothing. He had gone to Hungertobel under that name, he said. "Even if he had seen me at one time or another, he could hardly have recognized me. My illness has changed me."

The doctor laughed. "Are you trying to say you became ill in order to look for me here in Sonnenstein?"

Barlach did not answer.

Emmenberger directed at the old man a look full of sorrow. "My dear Commissioner," he continued, with a hint of reproach in his voice, "you really are most uncooperative in this interrogation."

"I'm the one to interrogate you, not the other way around," replied the Commissioner.

"You're breathing hard," Emmenberger said with concern.

Barlach no longer answered. Only the ticking of the clock could be heard, for the first time the old man was aware of it. Now I'll hear it again and again, he thought.

"Don't you think it's time to concede your defeat?" the doctor asked in a friendly manner.

"I don't have much choice," answered Barlach, dead-tired, putting his hands on the blanket. "The clock, if only it weren't for the clock."

"If only it weren't for the clock," the doctor repeated the old man's words. "Let's stop going around in circles. At seven o'clock I will kill you. That simplifies the case for you insofar as you can take with me an unbiased look at the case of Emmenberger versus Barlach. We're both scientists with opposing goals, chess players sitting in front of the same board. You made your move, now it's my turn. But this game has *one* peculiarity—either one of us will lose it or both. You've already lost your game. Now I'm curious to see whether I will have to lose mine."

"You will lose it," Barlach said softly.

Emmenberger laughed. "That's possible. I'd be a poor chess player if I didn't consider that possibility. But shall we take a closer look? You haven't got a chance—at seven I will come with my knives, and if, by luck, you do not die then, you will die in another year of your disease. But my chances—how do they look? Very bad, I admit. After all, you're already on my trail."

The doctor roared with laughter.

"You seem to be amused," the old man said, with surprise. The doctor seemed stranger and stranger all the time.

"I admit it amuses me to see myself fidget in your net like a fly, especially since you are simultaneously hanging in mine. But let us proceed. Who put you on my trail?"

The old man maintained that he had found it himself.

Emmenberger shook his head. "Let's talk about more credible things," he said. "One does not just sort of accidentally stumble upon my 'crimes'—to use this popular expression. And particularly not if one is a Commissioner of the City Police of Bern—as if I had stolen a bicycle or performed an abortion. Let's look at my case. You, who no longer have a chance, may hear the truth—the privilege of all who are condemned.

"I was cautious, meticulous, and thorough—I did a good job in this respect—but in spite of all caution there are, of course, certain circumstances that speak against me. A crime without some sort of circumstantial evidence is impossible in this world of chance. Let's enumerate. Where could Commissioner Hans Barlach enter in? There is, first of all, the picture in *Life*. I don't know who had the foolhardiness to take it in those days, but it is bad enough that it exists. However, we ought not to exaggerate. Millions have seen this famous picture, among them surely many who know me. And yet nobody has recognized me so far—the picture shows too little of my face. Who, then, could recognize me? Is it somebody who saw me in Stutthof and knows me here? An unlikely possibility. I have complete control over the people I took with me from there. But, as with any possibility, this one cannot be rejected outright. Or is it somebody who remembers me from my life in Switzerland before nineteen thirty-two? During that time I had a certain experience as a young student in a mountain hut—oh, I remember it very well—it happened under a red evening sky. Hungertobel was one of the five who were present then. It can therefore be assumed that Hungertobel was the one who recognized me."

"Nonsense," retorted the old man firmly. That was an unjustified conclusion, he went on, an empty speculation, nothing else. He sensed that his friend was threatened, yes, very much endangered, if he did not succeed in diverting all suspicion from him, though he could not quite imagine what this danger could be.

Emmenberger continued, his chin resting on his folded arms. "Let's not condemn poor old Doctor Hungertobel to death too fast. Instead, let's examine other possible circumstantial evidence against me; we shall try to get him off the hook. The affair with Nehle, for example. That too you found out, Commissioner. My congratulations! Doctor Marlok told me. Shall we admit it? I myself operated on Nehle to put the scar on his right eyebrow and the scald mark on his left forearm in order to make us identical, to make one out of two. I sent him to Chile under my name. And then I forced him, in a desolate, decrepit hotel room in Hamburg, to swallow a capsule of cyanide when he, the naïve nature boy who never did learn Latin and Greek, this amazing talent in the limitless field of medicine, returned—according to our agreement. C'est ça, as my beautiful mistress would say. Nehle was a gentleman. He submitted to his fate—a few determined blows on my part are hardly worth mentioning—and simulated the nicest suicide one could imagine. Let's not talk any more of this scene amidst whores and sailors, in the gray morning fog of a half-charred and rotten city, with the melancholy sound of lost ships in the background. This was a risky business which could still play extremely poor jokes on me. For what did I know about this talented dilettante's doings in Santiago, about the friendships he had there and who may suddenly appear here in Zurich to visit Nehle? But we want to stick to the facts.

"What evidence is there against me in the event somebody came upon this trail? There is, first of all, Nehle's ambitious idea of writing medical articles for *Lancet* and the *Swiss Medical Weekly*. They could prove to be fatal, provided somebody had the idea of undertaking stylistic comparisons with my own earlier articles. Nehle really wrote a much too uninhibited Berliner argot. But in order to do that, somebody would have to read the articles, which again points to a doctor. As you can see, things look grim for our friend. Of course, he is unsuspecting. We shall note that down in his favor. But when a criminologist allies with him—as I'm forced to assume— I can no longer give any guaranties for the old boy."

"I'm here on order of the police," the Commissioner stated calmly. "The German police have become suspicious of you and have asked the Berner police to investigate your case. You'll not operate on me tomorrow, for my death would convict you. Hungertobel, too, you will leave alone."

"Two after eleven," said the doctor.

"I can see," answered Barlach.

"The police—the police," continued Emmenberger, and looked at the sick man thoughtfully. "It is, of course, possible that even the police might find what is behind my life. However, in this case it seems to me to be most improbable because it would be by far the most favorable solution for you. The German police order the City Police of Bern to look for a criminal in Zurich! No, that does not seem logical to me. Maybe I would believe it if you were not sick, if it were not a matter of life and death with you. Your operation and your illness are not simulated, that I am in a position to decide as a doctor. Nor is your retirement from your office which the papers report. After all, what kind of a person are you? Most of all, a tough and stubborn old man, who dislikes giving up and dislikes stepping down, too. The possibility exists that you followed the call to arms privately, without any support, without the police—armed with your stretcher, so to speak, pursuing a vague suspicion you gained in a talk with Hungertobel, without any real proof. Maybe you were even too proud to tell anybody else besides Hungertobel your secret. Even he seems to be most uncertain of his case. All that mattered to you was to prove that even as a sick man you understood more than those

140

who retired you. I believe all this to be more probable than the possibility that the police will push a desperately sick man into such an unholy undertaking—especially since the police up to this hour have not hit the right trail in Fortschig's case, which they should have if they suspected me already. You were alone and you are proceeding against me alone, Commissioner. Even that vagabond writer was without any real notion of the facts, I believe."

"Why did you kill him?" cried the old man.

"Out of caution," the doctor replied indifferently. "Ten after eleven. Time flies, my friend, time flies. Out of caution I will have to kill Hungertobel, too."

"You want to kill him?" screamed the Commissioner, and tried to sit up.

"Lie down," Emmenberger ordered so firmly that the sick man obeyed. "Today is Thursday," he said. "All we doctors take a free afternoon on Thursday, don't we? So I decided to do Hungertobel and you and me a favor and asked him to visit us. He will come from Bern by car."

"What will happen?"

"Tom Thumb will sit in the back of his car," replied Emmenberger.

"The dwarf," moaned the Commissioner.

"The dwarf." The doctor nodded. "The dwarf again. A useful tool I brought home with me from Stutthof. It used to get between my feet, this silly thing, when

141

I operated. According to Herr Heinrich Himmler's federal laws I should have killed the little fellow as 'unworthy to live'—as if there were ever an Aryan giant worthier to live. I've always loved curiosities, and a deformed human being makes a most dependable tool. Because the little monkey sensed that he owed me his life, he let himself be trained most usefully."

The clock showed eleven-fourteen.

The Commissioner was so tired that his eyes closed for minutes at a time. And always when he opened them, he saw the clock, always the big round clock. He understood now that there was no escape for him. Emmenberger has seen through him. He was lost, and Hungertobel, too, was lost.

"You are a nihilist," he said softly, almost in a whisper, into the quiet room in which only the clock ticked. All the time.

"You're trying to say that I believe in nothing?" Emmenberger asked, and his voice betrayed no bitterness.

"I can't imagine that my words could have any other meaning," answered the old man in his bed, his hands helplessly on the blanket.

"In what do *you* believe, Commissioner?" asked the doctor. He did not move, but looked at the old man, curiously and tensely.

Barlach was silent.

In the background ticked the clock, without pause,

the clock, steady, with merciless hands, which pushed toward their goals.

"You are silent," Emmenberger said, and his voice had now lost the elegant, playful quality, and sounded clear and light. "You are silent. People of our time do not like to answer the question, 'What do you believe?' It's become bad taste to pose that question. One doesn't like to use big words, people say modestly. And least of all to give a definite answer—as for instance: I believe in God the Father, God the Son, and God the Holy Ghost, as the Christians once answered, proud that they could answer. One likes to be silent today when one is asked— like a girl to whom an embarrassing question has been put. Of course, one doesn't quite know either in what one actually does believe. It's by no means nothing. Good God no. One believes in something—even though it's quite vague, as if an uncertain fog hung over it all. One believes in something like humanity, Christianity, tolerance, justice, socialism, and love for one's neighbors— things that sound a little bit empty. People admit it, too, but they also think the words don't matter. What matters is to live decently and according to one's best conscience. And that they all try to do—partly by struggling for it, partly by just drifting. Everything we do, deeds and misdeeds, happens by chance. Good and evil fall into our lap like lottery tickets. By chance you become good and by chance you become evil. But they're always ready with

143

the big word *nihilist*. It's thrown—with much pathos and even more conviction—at those whom they fear.

"I know them, these people; they're convinced it's their right to maintain one plus one makes three, four, or ninety-nine, and that it would be unjust to demand of them the answer that one plus one is two. Anything clear appears narrow-minded to them, for clarity demands character. They have no notion that a determined Communist—to use a somewhat unusual example, for most Communists are Communists like most Christians are Christians, out of a misunderstanding—they have no notion, I say, that such a man who believes with his whole soul in the necessity of revolution and in the fact that only this road—though it may leave in its wake millions of corpses—will ultimately lead to salvation, to a better world, is much less of a nihilist than they. Than some Mr. Miller or Mr. Hoffman—who neither believes in a God nor disbelieves in one, but only in his right to make money —a belief which he is too cowardly to postulate as his credo. So they live like worms, with a foggy perception of something that is good and right and true—as if these things could exist in such a sticky mess."

"I had no idea that a hangman is capable of such a flood of words," said Barlach. "I had thought your kind to be rather tight-lipped."

"Bravo!" Emmenberger laughed. "You seem to be regaining your courage. Bravo! I need courageous people

144

for my experiments in my laboratory. And it's a pity that my object lessons always end with the death of the pupil. All right, let's see what kind of a belief I have and put it on a pair of scales, and then let's see which of us has the greater faith, when we put yours on the other side. I, the nihilist—since you call me that—or you, the Christian. You came to me in the name of humanity or whatever other ideals, in order to destroy me. I think you can hardly reject my curiosity."

"I understand," answered the Commissioner. He tried to keep down the fear that rose in him—more and more threatening, more and more gigantic—with each movement of the hands of the clock. "Now you want to grind out your credo. Strange that even mass murderers have one."

"It is after eleven o'clock," replied Emmenberger.

"How kind of you to remind me," groaned the old man, shaking with rage and helplessness.

"Man—what is man?" The doctor laughed. "I'm not ashamed to have a credo, I'm not silent as you were silent. Like the Christians, who believe in three things which are only one thing—the Trinity—I believe in two things which are one and the same, namely that something is and that I am. I believe in matter, which is *simultaneously* energy and mass, an incomprehensible universe and a globe, around which we can walk and which we can feel is like a child's ball, on which we live and drift through the adventurous emptiness of space. I believe in matter (how shabby and empty it is by comparison to say, 'I believe in a God')—matter that is seizable as animal, as plant, or as coal, and not seizable, hardly calculable, as atom. It needs no God or whatever else is invented for it. Its only incomprehensible mystery is its being. And I believe that I am, a particle of this matter, atom, energy, mass, molecule—as you are—and that my existence gives me the right to do what I want. As a particle, I constitute only a moment, a mere incident, just as life in this gigantic world is only one of matter's immeasurable possibilities, as much chance as I am—if the earth were a little closer to the sun, there would be no life—and my purpose consists of *only* being a moment. Oh, the tremendous night when I understood this! Nothing is holy but matter: man, animal, plant, the moon, the Milky Way, whatever I see, are accidental groupings, nonessentials, as the form of the waves of the water are something nonessential. It is indifferent whether things are or are not. They are interchangeable. If they are not, something else exists. When life on this planet dies out, it will appear somewhere in the universe on another planet. It is ridiculous to attribute permanence to man, for it will always be only the illusion of permanence. It is ridiculous to invent systems of power in order to vegetate for a few years as the head of some state or some church. It is senseless to strive for the welfare of man in a world structured like a lottery—as if it would make sense to have each ticket win a penny, as if there existed another yearning but this one —*for once* to be the singular, sole, unjust man who wins the whole lottery. It is nonsense to believe in matter and *at the same time* in humanism. One can only believe in matter and the I. There is no justice. How could matter be just? There is only freedom, which cannot be earned —for then there would have to be a justice; which cannot be given—for who could give it?—which can only be taken. Freedom is the courage to commit crime, for freedom itself is a crime."

"I understand," cried the Commissioner, shaking, a dying animal, lying on his white sheet as if on the edge of an endless, indifferent road. "You believe in nothing but the right to torture man."

"Bravo!" answered the doctor, and clapped his hands. "Bravo! I call him a good pupil who dares to deduce the law under which I live. Bravo, bravo!" (And again he clapped his hands.) "I dared to be myself and nothing, nothing else. I devoted myself to that which made me free—murder and torture. For when I kill another human being—and I will do it again at seven—when I put myself outside all the order of this world, erected by our weakness—I become free, I become nothing but a moment. But what a moment! In intensity as gigantic, as powerful, as unjustified as matter. And the screams and the pain which flood toward me from glassy eyes and open mouths, the convulsing, impotent white flesh under my knife, reflect my triumph and my freedom and nothing else."

He fell silent. Slowly he rose and sat down on the operating table.

Above him the clock showed three minutes to twelve, two minutes to twelve, twelve.

"Seven hours," Barlach whispered, almost inaudibly, from the bed.

"Now show me your belief," said Emmenberger. His voice was calm again and without emotion, no longer passionate and hard, as it had been toward the end of his long speech.

Barlach answered nothing.

"You are silent," said the doctor. "Again and again you are silent."

The sick man gave no answer.

"You are silent and silent," stated the doctor, and put both hands on the operating table. "Unconditionally I put everything on one card. I was powerful because I was never afraid, because it made no difference to me whether I was discovered or not. I am even now prepared to gamble. I shall concede my defeat if you, Commissioner, can prove to me that you have a faith as great, as unconditional as mine."

The old man was silent.

"Say something," Emmenberger continued after a

148

pause, while he looked tensely and greedily at the sick man. "Give me an answer. You're a Christian. You were baptized. Say, 'I believe with a certainty, with a power that overshadows the belief of a shameless murderer in matter like a sun of light overshadows a pitiful winter moon.' Or say at least, 'I believe with a power that equals his, in Christ, who is God's Son.'"

The clock ticked in the background.

"Maybe this belief is too difficult," said Emmenberger, for still Barlach was silent, and he stepped to the old man's bed. "Maybe you have an easier, more popular belief. Say, 'I believe in justice and in the humanity this justice is to serve. For its sake, and *only* for its sake have I, old and sick, taken it upon me to come here—without giving a thought to fame and triumph of my person over others.' Say it, it is an easy, decent belief, which we can still demand of today's mankind, say it and you are free. I will be satisfied with your belief, and when you say it, I will think that you have a belief as great as mine."

The old man was silent.

"Maybe you don't believe that I will let you go?" asked Emmenberger.

No answer.

"Say it anyway," the doctor ordered the old man. "Confess your belief even if you do not trust my words. Maybe you can only be saved if you have a belief. Maybe now is your *last chance*, the chance not only to save yourself but Hungertobel as well. There is still time to phone him. You have found me and I, you. Someday my game will be over, somewhere the accounts won't balance. Why should I not be the one to lose? I can kill you—I can let you go, which means my death. I have reached a point from which I can deal with myself as with a strange person. I destroy myself—I save myself."

He stopped and looked at the Commissioner. "It does not matter what I do," he said, "a more powerful position cannot be attained. To conquer this Point of Archimedes is the highest that man can win for himself. It is his only sense in the nonsense of this world, in the mystery of this dead matter, which again and again creates out of itself life and death, like a carrion. But I bind—that is my malice—your escape to a silly joke, a childishly simple condition, that you can show me a faith as great as mine. Show it! The belief in goodness ought to be as strong in man as the belief in evil! Show it! Nothing will amuse me more than to watch my own ride to hell."

Only the clock could be heard.

"Then say it for the cause," Emmenberger continued after some while, "for the belief in God's Son, the belief in justice."

The clock, nothing but the clock.

"Your faith!" screamed the doctor. "Show me your faith!"

The old man was lying there, his hands clutching the blankets.

150

"Your faith! Your faith!" Emmenberger's voice was like bronze, like trumpet blasts, breaking through an endless gray sky.

The old man was silent.

Then Emmenberger's face—which had been greedy for an answer—became cold and relaxed. Only the scar above the right eye was reddened. It was as if disgust shook him when he turned away from the sick man, tired and indifferent. He walked through the door, which closed softly, so that the Commissioner was enveloped by the gleaming blue of the room, in which only the round disk of the clock continued to tick as if it were the old man's heart.

A NURSERY RHYME

AND so Barlach lay there and waited for death. Time passed, the hands of the clock turned round, covered each other, separated again. Then it was twelve-thirty, one, five after one, twenty to two, two o'clock, ten after two, two-thirty. The room seemed suspended, motionless, dead space in the shadowless blue light, the cupboards full of strange instruments behind the glass which vaguely reflected Barlach's face and hands. Everything was there, the white operating table, Dürer's painting with the mighty, rigid horse, the metal plate across the window, the empty chair with its back toward the old man— nothing alive except the mechanical *tick-tock* of the clock. Now it was three o'clock, then four. No noise, no moans, no talk, no screams, no steps, penetrated to the old man, who lay there on a metal bed, who did not move, whose body hardly rose and fell. There was no longer an outside world, no earth that revolved, no sun, and no city. There was nothing but a greenish round disk with hands that moved, overtook each other, covered each other, tore away from each other. It was four-thirty, twenty-five to five, thirteen to five, five, one after five, two after five, three after five, four after five, six after five. Barlach had painfully managed to sit up. He rang the bell once, twice, a few times. He waited. Maybe he could yet talk to Nurse Clari. Maybe an accident could save him. Five-thirty.

Carefully he twisted his body around. Then he fell. For a long time he stayed in front of the bed on a red carpet, and above him, somewhere above the glass cupboards, the clock ticked, the hands pushed on—thirteen to six, twelve to six, eleven to six. Then he crawled slowly toward the door, reached it, tried to get up, to clutch the knob, fell back, stayed on the floor, tried it once more, a third time, a fifth time. In vain. He scratched on the door, for he was too weak to hammer at it with his fists. Like a rat, he thought. Then he stayed motionless again, crawled back into the room, looked at the clock. Ten after six. "Another fifty minutes," he said, loud and clear in the silence, so that it frightened him. "Fifty minutes."

He wanted to crawl back into bed, but he felt that he no longer had the power. So he stayed on the floor, in front of the operating table, and waited. Around him were the room, the cupboards, the knives, the bed, the clock—again and again the clock, a burned sun in a blue rotting universe, a ticking idol, a face without a mouth, or eyes, or nose—but with two wrinkles that pulled together, became one—twenty-five to seven, twenty-two to seven—that did not seem to separate any more, that separated now after all—twenty-one to seven, twenty to seven, nineteen to seven. Time passed, marched on, in the impartial rhythm of the clock. Ten to seven.

Barlach sat up, leaned against the operating table—an old sick man, alone and helpless. He grew calm. Behind him was the clock and in front of him the door. He stared at it, resigned and humble, this rectangle through which *he* must come, *he* who would kill him, slowly and methodically like a clock, skillfully cutting with the gleaming knives. And so he sat. Now he himself had become time, he was the ticking—he needed no longer to look at the clock, now he knew that he only had to wait for minutes, for three, for two—now he counted the seconds, which were one with the beating of his heart, a hundred yet, sixty yet, thirty yet. So he counted, babbling with white bloodless lips; so he stared, a living clock, at the door, which opened now, at seven, all at once, offering him the vision of a black hell, an opened gorge. In its middle he sensed vaguely a gigantic dark figure, but it was not Emmenberger, as the old man believed. For out of the gaping abyss roared sarcastically and hoarsely an old children's tune.

> "Little Hans
> Went alone
> Into the big black forest!"

sang a screechy voice. Filling the doorframe, mighty and powerful, in a black caftan hanging, torn, from huge limbs, stood the Jew Gulliver.

"Greetings, Commissar," said the giant, and closed the door. "So here I find you again, you sad knight *sans peur et sans reproche*, who went out to slay the evil dragon with the force of his spirit, sitting in front of a trestle similar to the one onto which I was once chained in the pretty village of Stutthof near Danzig." And he lifted the old man so that he rested against his chest like a child, and put him to bed.

"Greetings." He laughed when the Commissioner still could not find words, but rested there, pale as death; then he pulled a bottle and two glasses out of the tatters of his caftan.

"I don't have vodka any more," said the Jew as he filled the glasses and sat down on the bed. "But in a rundown farmhouse somewhere in the Emmenvalley, a hole full of darkness and snow, I stole a few dusty bottles of this valiant potato brandy. It will do. One has to be lenient with a dead man, right, Commissar? When a corpse like myself—a firewater corpse, so to speak—fetches its tribute from the living in night and fog before crawling back into its cellar, it is perfectly in order. Here, Commissar, drink."

He put the glass to Barlach's lips, and the old man drank. It felt good, even though he thought it was hardly the proper medicine.

"Gulliver," he whispered, and groped for the other's

hand. "How could you know that I was in this cursed mousetrap?"

The giant laughed. "Christian," he answered, and the hard eyes in his scar-covered naked skull gleamed (he had drunk a few glasses meanwhile), "why else did you call me into the Salem? I knew right away that you had a suspicion, that maybe the inestimable possibility existed of finding this Nehle still among the living. I did not believe for a moment it was only psychological interest which made you ask after Nehle, as you maintained in that night full of vodka. Should I have let you go down the road to ruin alone? Today we no longer can fight evil alone, like the knights used to once upon a time with some dragon or other. The times are past where it is enough to be a little bit sharp in order to catch the criminals we are dealing with. You fool of a detective! Time itself has led you *ad absurdum*. From then on I never let you out of my sight again, and last night I appeared to the good Doctor Hungertobel in person. I really had to work to get him out of his fainting spell, he was so afraid. But then I knew what I wanted to know, and now I am here to get things back into their old order. For you the mice of Bern, for me the rats of Stutthof. That is the division of the world."

"How did you get here?" Barlach asked in a whisper.

The giant's face broke into a grin. "Not hidden under some seat of the Swiss Railroads, as you are thinking," he replied, "but in Hungertobel's car."

"He's alive?" asked the old man, who had finally

regained his composure and stared breathlessly at the Jew.

"He'll take you back to the old familiar Salem in a few minutes," said the Jew, and drank the potato schnapps in huge gulps. "He's waiting outside in the car."

"The dwarf," Barlach screamed, pale as death, at his sudden recognition that the Jew could know nothing of this danger. "The dwarf! He will kill him!"

"Yes, the dwarf." The giant laughed, still drinking, frightening in his wild raggedness, and he whistled through the fingers of his right hand, shrill and piercing, as one whistles a dog. Then the metal plate across the window was pushed up. Like a monkey a little black shadow somersaulted into the room, uttering unintelligible gurgling sounds, glided fast as lightning toward Gulliver, and jumped up on his lap, pressing the ugly, old dwarfed face against the Jew's torn chest and clutching with his little crippled arms Gulliver's mighty head.

"There you are, my monkey, my little animal, my little monster," the Jew fondled the dwarf with a singing voice. "My poor Minotaur, my tortured little puppy, you who so often whined yourself to sleep in my arms, you only companion of my poor soul during those blood-filled nights in Stutthof. You my son, my mandrake root. My crippled Argos, on his endless wanderings Odysseus has come back to you. Oh, I thought that you were the one who sent the poor drunk Fortschig into another life, that you glided into his light shaft. Did not the evil witch-master Nehle or Emmenberger or whatever his name

158

train you for such feats in our torture camp? Here, bite
into my finger, my puppy. And as I am in the car, sitting
next to Hungertobel, I hear a happy whining behind me,
like that of a mangy cat. It was my poor little friend,
Commissar, whom my fist pulled out from under the seat.
What do we want to do with this little animal now, this
animal that is nevertheless a human being, this little fellow
that was degraded to an animal, this little murderer who
alone of us all is innocent and who reflects in his sad
brown eyes the misery of all living creatures?"

The old man had sat up in his bed and looked at the
ghostlike pair, at this tortured Jew and at the dwarf,
whom the giant let dance on his knees like a child.

"And Emmenberger?" he asked. "What about Emmenberger?" for a moment, the giant's face became like a
gray primeval stone, into which the scars had been ham-
mered as with a chisel. He flung the empty bottle with a
swing of his huge arms toward the cupboards, splintering
their glass—so that the dwarf, squealing like a frightened
rat, hid with one jump under the operating table.

"Why do you ask, Commissar?" hissed the Jew, but
at once he controlled himself—only the terrible slits of
his eyes gleamed dangerously—and slowly he pulled a
second bottle from his caftan and began to drink again in
wild gulps. "It makes one thirsty to live in a hell. Love
your enemies as thyself, someone said on the stony hill of
Golgotha, and had himself nailed to the cross, hanging
on its rotten wood, a piece of cloth flapping around his

hips. Pray for Emmenberger's poor soul, Christian, Jehovah likes only the daring prayers. Pray! He is no longer—he after whom you ask. My trade is bloody, Commissar, I must not think of theological studies when I pursue my work. I was just according to the laws of Moses, just according to my God, Commissar. I have killed him, as Nehle was killed once in some damp hotel room, and the police will just as infallibly conclude a suicide now as they concluded then. What shall I tell you? My hand led his; clutched in my arms, he pressed the fatal capsule between his teeth. Ahasuerus's mouth is taciturn and his bloodless lips will remain closed. What went on between us, between the Jew and his torturer, and how the roles had to be reversed according to the law of justice, how I became the torturer and he the victim shall—aside from us two—be known only to God, who allowed it all to happen. We must bid farewell, Commissar."

The giant rose.

"What will happen now?" whispered Barlach.

"Nothing will happen," answered the Jew. He grabbed the old man by the shoulders and jerked him forward, so that their faces were close together, one's eyes reflecting the other's. "Nothing will happen, nothing," whispered the giant once more. "Nobody—except you and Hungertobel—knows that I was here; inaudibly I glided, a shadow, through the corridors, to Emmenberger, to you—nobody knows that I exist, only the poor devils that I save, a handful of Jews, a handful of Christians. Let the world bury Emmenberger and let the newspapers write the eulogistic obituaries with which they will commemorate this dead man. The Nazis wanted Stutthof, the millionaires, this clinic. Others will want other things. We as individuals cannot save this world, that would be so hopeless a task as that of poor Sisyphus. Is was not given into our hands, and not into those of a mighty person or a people or of the devil—even though he is the most powerful of us all—but into God's hands, who makes His decisions alone. We can help only in single instances, not in the whole—the limitation of the poor Jew Gulliver, the limitation of all people. Therefore, we ought not to try to save the world but to get through it—the only true adventure that remains for us at this late hour." And carefully, like a father with a child, the giant lowered the old man into his bed.

"Come on, my monkey," Gulliver called, and whistled. With one mighty jump, squealing and babbling, the dwarf shot up and settled on the Jew's left shoulder.

"That's right, my little murderer," the giant praised him. "We two will stay together. After all, we are both cast out of human company—you by nature and I because I belong to the dead. Farewell, Commissar, we are off to a nocturnal visit in the wide Russian plain, off to dare a new sinister descent into the catacombs of this world, into the lost holes of those who are persecuted by the mighty ones."

Once again the Jew waved to the old man, then he reached with both hands into the bars, bent them apart, and lowered himself out of the window.

"Farewell, Commissar." He laughed once more with his strangely singing voice. Only his shoulders and the huge naked head were visible, against his left cheek the dwarf's old face, while the almost full moon appeared on the other side of his majestic head, so that it seemed as if the Jew carried on his shoulders the whole universe, earth and humanity. "Farewell, my knight *sans peur et sans reproche*, my Barlach," he said. "Gulliver moves on to the giants and dwarfs, to other countries, other worlds, evermore, always. Farewell, Commissar, farewell," and with the last farewell, he had disappeared.

The old man closed his eyes. A feeling of peace surged through him. Especially since he knew that Hungertobel was now standing in the softly opening door— to bring him back to Bern.